The Enchanted

AN INCREDIBLE TALE

The

Enchanted

AN INCREDIBLE TALE

by Elizabeth Coatsworth

Illustrated by Mary Frank

Pantheon Books

ALSO BY ELIZABETH COATSWORTH:

Here I Stay
The Hand of Apollo
Jock's Island
Door to the North
The Last Fort
Sword of the Wilderness
Down Half the World
The Captain's Daughter
Jon the Unlucky
The Place
The Princess and the Lion
The Cat Who Went to Heaven

Library of Congress Catalog Card Number: 68-12652

Manufactured in the United States of America

CONTENTS

The Enchanted

AN INCREDIBLE TALE

T here is in northern Maine a township or, as they say here, a "plantation," called the Enchanted. It lies in the heart of the forest country and is seldom entered except by lumbermen bound for some winter logging camp from which they return with curious stories. There is a stream in this forest which disappears underground and then reappears again. It is known as the Upper and Lower Enchanted, but whether the plantation is called for the stream or the stream for the plantation it would be hard to say now, so many years after their naming.

I

David Ross had never heard of either stream
or plantation when he bought a semi-deserted
farm on a clearing on the Dead River. It was
marginal land with a vengeance, and he knew
that he would be wise to keep away and let the
young pines and hemlocks have the old fields
which they had begun to make their nursery.
But something in the land pleased him. On one
side lay the shallow and rapid Dead River with
its unbroken wilderness look. Then came the
bench of cleared land, the rutted road, the farm
buildings, still relatively sound, and then narrow fields and forest again: spruce, hemlock,
arborvitae and pine, scattered with groves of
hardwoods whose paler leaves seemed like
patches of sunlight on the hills.

He was too near the mountains to see them,
but he felt their presences beyond the trees. He
had seen them from the tops of hills some distance back on the road to Canada, and he was
aware of their shapes, like blue waves of land
rising out of the forest.

"Pretty lonely here," said the real-estate man
who was showing him the place. "The last man
raised horses for the lumber companies and
boarded their stock summers. That's why the
barn's so big. He did well, I believe, but his wife

had a nervous breakdown and he took her back to her people in Portland. The place has been listed a couple of years now, and he's come down a good deal from his original price."

David was looking about and said nothing, and after a pause the real-estate man added with a suddenly confidential air:

"Fact is, I believe you could get it for a couple of hundred less than the price, if you make an offer."

"I'll look around," said David. "Don't bother to come. The ground's pretty soggy. Just let me have the key if you will."

More than willing, the real-estate man settled down in his seat behind the wheel of the car to read his paper and smoke a cigarette. He had been showing farms all spring and the best ones, nearer the towns, had all been bought. People seemed crazy to own land—at least the ones who came to him were. This Ross boy was a nice boy, pleasant looking, with his sandy hair and narrow gray eyes. Not much of a talker, but what he said was to the point and he seemed self-reliant. This Dead River Farm was no place for a jumpy man. The real-estate dealer swept it with a practiced eye.

"If I had to live here, I'd go nuts," he thought

and turned his attention to the paper and the horse-racing scores.

David Ross was glad to be alone. He walked down to the river, smelling the wet earth and the odor of new green coming up through old leaves which still had their own autumn mustiness. The land had not been long abandoned. It had a shaggy look, for the fields had not been cut for over a year, but the clumps of alders by the river, the squat soft-needled young pines here and there were all small, and would not be hard to root out. Two mergansers rose and beat up river as he approached. The spray caught the light, where their wings had struck the surface as they took flight.

The house was simple but pleasant. It had been painted white some years before, but David saw it as red. There was a porch along one side and an ell. He went in by the kitchen door, which stuck and groaned against the weight of his shoulder and then suddenly yielded. Sink, pump, wood stove were in place and there were even dishes still on the shelves. In the parlor, squirrels had made a nest in the sofa and the rug had been chewed up. The room smelled stale, but it faced south. The sun shone in through windows looking down towards the river. There was a bedroom across the hall and two more up the stairs. The wallpapers were peeling in places—paint would be better, at least at first. He went into the shed. Half a woodpile had been left there, the butt ends fitted into a neat mosaic. The woodpile suddenly made him feel at home, as though he belonged. He could light a fire anytime, right now if he chose, but he stifled the impulse and went out to look at the barn.

The barn was large and there were stalls along each side littered still with old straw and manure changed almost to dust. There was still hay, darkened by age, in the lofts over the stalls, and swallows flew in and out of a broken light in the window at the gable end, building their plastered nests against the beams. A hayrack was suspended above his head in the open center of the barn. Its wheels were a cheerful wagon-blue and looked as though they had been painted yesterday.

There was a well at one side of the house. The cover would have to be renewed, but David remembered seeing a pail and rope in the shed and brought them out. The bucket went down a long way and he spilled half the contents as he pulled it up. He drank slowly of the cold clear water. He was the first to disturb those black depths for two years he supposed. The taste pleased him. It was the first gift from his farm, for as he drank, without conscious decision, he thought, "I'll take it."

Still he made a brief tour of the upper fields. There were some apple trees back of the house, not in good condition, but they looked hardy and had plenty of blossoms. The remnants of a path led past a thicket of raspberries, and he could see that there had been a garden. A very small stream ran along one side of it, crossed by a plank, and beyond he found the spring house, which was something he hadn't expected. The fields were a little more overgrown on this side nearer the forest. By the wall he saw a fox which had been catching mice in the grass. It paused, lifted one paw and cocked its ears, studying him, and then streaked over the wall and disappeared. There were a few more stones than in the lower fields, but not many. This had all been river bottom once, good land, but remote, wilderness land with the wilderness always trying to reclaim it the moment it had a chance.

His tour brought him to the car where the

agent had finished his paper and was now dozing in the sun with his head tipped back and his mouth open.

"If I can arrange with any of the lumber companies to board their horses, I'll make an offer," David told him.

The other man yawned and sat up suddenly, straightening his coat and tie.

"O.K., Mr. Ross," he said. "You don't think you may find it a little lonesome?"

"I feel now I wouldn't mind being alone for a while. I've been living pretty close to a lot of people."

"You're not a married man, I take it?" the real-estate man went on, after he had turned the car in the overgrown drive. "Well, it might do for an unmarried man, for a while anyhow. You could have a radio with a battery to listen to evenings. I believe there's a family beyond at the end of the road. And someone's living in the cabin we passed, just this side."

"Yes," said David, "there's smoke coming from the stove pipe and I noticed chickens. No woman there to judge by what's on the line."

"Well, there are plenty of girls at the other place, I hear."

David laughed.

"I didn't come here to get a girl."

But no one's eyes are open to his fate. A man may step from his house intending no more than to buy shaving soap at the corner drugstore, and return with his entire life changed, or perhaps never return at all.

It took nearly two weeks to get in touch with some of the lumber companies and to look up the title and sign the deeds. Ross found plenty of cooperation from the lumber people whom he saw at Skowhegan. They had in the past found Dead River Farm very conveniently near the camps.

"It will take you most of the summer to get things in running order again," Mr. Jordan, the manager of one of the biggest companies, told him, "and for this year we've made other arrangements. But next season we'll plan to leave as many teams with you as you can handle. It saves trucking them out. How are you off for money? We'll be glad to lend you some if you need it, after looking over the situation with you."

"Thanks," said David. "No, I'm all right so far. But I'll remember."

Ed Jordan had been most friendly and businesslike, and David felt heartened by his encouragement. But he intended to run his farm on his own lines, without silent partners. He didn't know much about farming, although he had spent a few summers on a farm as a boy and had learned to milk, harness a horse, pull weeds and help with the haying. That would do for a starter.

He went to the Skowhegan library and took out a book on horse breeding and doctoring and some government pamphlets on hay and horse raising. In his bleak hotel bedroom he read evenings until late and now and then jotted down some name or fact in a pocket notebook he bought for the purpose, but most of the information he stored away in his head, getting the feel of the subject.

When the deeds were signed, he made inquiries about horses and asked the local veterinarian for advice. With his aid, he bought a team of strawberry roans for his own use, at least to begin with. They were part Percheron and heavy enough for hauling in the woods.

"Better than average for the price," the veterinarian told him. "But we'll have to go further before we find the right mare. She's more important if she's to be the beginning of your stock farm. Better begin right."

The mare David bought did not seem to him a very good-looking animal. He was shown many prettier ones, but his adviser swept them aside.

"Alice is the one you want," he explained. "She's at least ten years old and that's why she's in your price range. But I know her colts, and there's never been a weak-backed or weak-kneed one in the lot. She's been bred already and right, so you don't have that to think of."

Alice laid back her ears and gave Dave a mean look. She was standing with one hip thrown out and her underlip drooped. Dave looked at her with an eye as unadmiring as her own, but he trusted the veterinarian and bought her.

When he arrived back at Dead River Farm early in June, he headed a small caravan. His own car was overflowing with supplies and tools, a new mattress, a new pump, a roll of barbed wire, and some kitchen equipment. Behind came a truck with Patrick and Patience—he had kept the names—then another truck with Alice and Meadow Maid, the half Jersey, half Guernsey cow, tied as far away from one another as possible with a wooden slide between them because of Alice's temper.

As they passed the tar-paper shack at the edge of the clearing, a small grizzled man opened the door and stood watching them. When Dave raised his hand in greeting, the stranger made a brief answering gesture. "My nearest neighbor," thought Dave. "I must go over soon and get acquainted."

But for the first days he was too tired to want to get acquainted with anything but his bed when the June darkness came at last. He had made out a list of things to be done—"first things first," he reminded himself grimly. "And that means getting the garden plowed and seeds in before I wake up and find that summer's half gone and it's too late."

For the next week he was as busy as a man can be, working from dawn until he could no longer see in the darkness. His body ached in every joint and his eyes were bloodshot with weariness, but a kind of excitement kept him going. He was learning all the time, for he began by doing everything the hard way. His successes buoyed him up, his failures depressed him, but he went ahead through successes and failures, and as the days passed, he could feel his body slowly hardening until he began to wake up less exhausted in the mornings.

🌿 Spring

Some day it would rain and then it would be time enough to begin work on the house. Its dust and stains and confusions bothered him, but he had determined to give his first effort to the land, and give it he did, straightening old fence posts and renewing them; stringing new wire where the old was broken through; slashing and hauling at young alder thickets and new-born pines; carrying rocks from the upper hayfields to the walls.

"Whatever else a New England field raises, you can count every spring on a new crop of rocks," he thought. It was a great day when he had the pasture tight and ready for the animals, and with a feeling of real triumph he saw them saunter out into the sunlight as he put up the bars behind them. The pasture was damp and misted over in places with the last bluets, and there were strawberry blossoms and young berries just reddening everywhere underfoot.

He stood for a moment watching his stock snatch for the first time at grass in what was to be their own pasture, and just then his ear caught the sound of a horse coming down the road from beyond his house. The air was almost windless and Dave could hear a chattering and murmuring like that of a covey of birds above and below and through the slow trample of hoofs and creak of wheels. Then an old canopied surrey appeared, pulled in a leisurely fashion by a black horse, which ambled along, half asleep. A small middle-aged man was driving, squeezed over into one corner by a boy and a couple of plump black-eyed girls. The back seat seemed to contain another pair of girls and of boys, too, and they were all talking and laughing at once, but in low voices. When they saw Dave, the young people waved and called out cheerfully, and the father flourished the whip which he carried unused in his right hand. One of the roans neighed and the old black horse halted, pricked its ears, surveyed the strangers, and then in silence went shuffling on, the dust puffing up from the road with every step.

Slowly the vehicle passed out of sight and into the woods while Dave stared after it. These must be his neighbors down the road. It was hard to believe that they were all one family—they seemed so much of an age—yet there was no doubt but that they were. They looked alike. He had never felt such a sense of family as in those few minutes when he stood watching the old surrey go by, overflowing with life, so many individuals and yet unified by common blood and interests.

"Well," he said to himself a little taken aback by their numbers, "must be French Canadians," and with a final glance at the roans feeding close together as became harness mates, and Alice at the far end of the pasture switching flies with vicious intensity, and the young cow acting as though she had grazed here all her life, he went off whistling to get his potatoes into the ground.

All day Dave was more occupied than usual with his thoughts. He couldn't get that lively crowd out of his mind. There certainly were girls enough and they were pretty if you liked that kind. They didn't look like town girls. They were old-fashioned, round and smiling. They looked as though they knew how to make apple pies and patchwork quilts, and they seemed to giggle a lot, and nudge each other and duck their heads.

He was ditching a place in the lower hayfield that afternoon and kept his eyes and ears open for their return, but he saw nothing of them until he was eating a late supper by lamplight and then he heard them passing. They were in as high spirits as ever, but their voices were muted a little, perhaps by the dusk.

Following an unexpected impulse, he opened the front door and waved. They saw him outlined by lamplight and called back. He hadn't noticed before what sweet voices the girls had. One of the boys must have whistled, and the others took it up.

After they were gone, Dave still stood looking out. The evening star hung in a green sky in the direction they were taking. He could see the ridged wall of the forest dark below it. The murmur of the river came up to him from across the fields where he had sweated all day alone in the sun. His feelings were too much for him, and he decided to take his lantern and walk over to call on his nearest neighbor, the solitary in the tar-paper shack.

He quickly washed his dishes in a pail, shut off the draughts in the stove, and went out, after a glance at Meadow Maid in her stanchions. He had milked her before supper and the horses he had left out in the pasture. They were too heavy to be attacked by bears, the veterinarian had told him. When he had colts, it would be a different matter.

His lantern swung along, one more light among so many. There were thousands of stars overhead, and fireflies in the lower land by the river. He could see two unwinking windows, looking like owl's eyes across the fields, and knew that his neighbor must be at home.

🕊 Spring

As he drew near the shack, the door opened and the man came out to meet him.

"He has good ears," Dave thought and held out his hand, which the other shook warmly.

"Come in, come in," the stranger urged. "I've been hoping you'd come over when you had the time. I'm not much of a visitor myself, but I like to have a friend drop in to see me."

The room inside was narrow and neat. A stove, two kitchen chairs, a kitchen table covered with red oilcloth, and a cot completed its furnishings and there were a few pans, a washbasin, a calendar on the wall, and some clothes hung on homemade hooks. Two axes stood leaning in a corner below the clothes.

"My name's John Chandler," the stranger said, "and I guess you're Ross. Sit you, sit you. If you find it too warm, kick open the door beside you."

Dave was aware of a keen, somehow quizzical appraisal. Chandler offered him tobacco and filled his own pipe.

"See you brought along an extra mare. Guess you plan to raise horses, too, like the last fellow."

Dave nodded. He was never much of a talker and now he answered briefly without enlargement.

Chandler was more talkative.

"I know more about horses than about cows. They don't have cows at lumber camps, but I've driven plenty of teams. Know anything about shoeing? I can help you out sometime if you need a horse shod in a hurry."

They smoked for a little while in silence. Finally Dave said:

"You're a lumberman, Mr. Chandler?"

The little man grinned. "Everyone calls me 'Chip.' Yes, I've been a lumberman all my days. Was born in the woods; but I'm getting too old for it now. I'm older than I look by a long shot. So I built me a house here in the open and putter around a little. Raise a few hens and garden and cut firewood and shoot a deer now and again. I get along."

"Who are the people down the road?" David asked.

Chip gave him a quick look, and said noncommittally:

"They call themselves 'Perdry.'"

"Perdry," Dave repeated after him. "I thought they might be French Canadians."

Chip shrugged and Dave noticed for the first time the suspenders he wore over his faded red shirt.

Spring

"I don't think they call themselves French Canadians," he said.

The conversation seemed to Dave to have grown rather laconic.

"I noticed them drive by today," he tried again. "They seemed like good people."

Chip gave a queer snort, which might have been of laughter.

"Lots of pretty girls," he exclaimed, almost with a jeer. "Quite a sight they make."

"He's a woman-hater," Dave thought. "An old natural-born bachelor," and he said more easily:

"Yes, they are pretty. They all look alike."

Chip snorted again.

"I'll say they look alike. When you have anything to do with the Perdrys, watch your step."

"You mean they aren't honest?"

"Oh, they're honest enough. No, I've said my say. Just go slow," and the older man would say no more.

Dave stayed a little longer talking about other things. The lumberman knew a great deal about the woods.

"There's fine timber all back in here. Boy, the first growth spruce I've seen back in the Enchanted! *And* pines. They rise up like they'd never stop. There's a stand of pine over by Upper Enchanted Stream I've never seen matched and they haven't been touched yet—"

"What do you mean, Enchanted?" Dave asked, his attention caught by the word.

"I mean Enchanted," the older man said emphatically. "You can see it on the maps. It's the name of the plantation. Didn't you know that you bought at the edge of the Enchanted? Well, you did. All that's the Enchanted, and don't you forget it," and he waved his hand towards the back of the room, the cot, the calendar and the silent black forest outside rising tier upon tier towards the stars.

"Where did it get that name?" Dave asked, and Chip looked at him almost slyly. How much should he tell? How much would the other man believe? He said:

"There's plenty of reasons for the name. Queer things happen in all the woods, things no one would believe who hadn't been there. But the queerest things happen in the Enchanted, and they're still happening—why, right now—" But suddenly he broke off, stared at Dave, and shook his head doubtfully. When he went on, it was in a different tone of voice. "Ever heard of the stream? It disappears underground, but you can still hear it."

"That doesn't seem so queer," Dave remarked, as Chip paused. "I've known brooks do that."

"The Enchanted's different. It don't seem so much like water as singing. Sometimes the whole woods sound with it. You ask anyone who's lumbered in the Enchanted. It's like voices sometimes. The men generally work together."

"What do the voices do?"

Chip gave him a black look. "Sometimes they scream. I was at a camp in 1904 up in there. One night we heard someone scream. We all listened and it screamed again. We got lanterns and went out looking for the man in trouble. There was new snow on the ground that had fallen since we came in from work. We hunted that night and most of the next day and we never found so much as a man's footprint."

He looked at Dave, who nodded. Dave knew that he would be wise to say nothing, but he couldn't resist asking:

"Couldn't it have been a Canada lynx?"

"We was sung to sleep in our cradles by Canada lynxes."

There was another pause. A billet turned uneasily in the fire box and the smoke from the two pipes rose and mingled tranquilly in the hot air of the cabin. Dave felt sleepy and looked at his lantern, but Chip had started again.

"I suppose you wouldn't call it queer if you chased a buck into a thicket and it come out the other side a big black bear? I knew a man that happened to once."

The devil of reasonableness was clamoring in Dave's head. He knew that every one of his remarks was antagonizing Chip, but he couldn't help making them.

"I'd think there was both a buck and a bear in the thicket and that the bear came out first."

To his surprise, the old lumberman remained quite calm this time; he made no answer as he tapped the tobacco out of his pipe against the stove.

"Yes," he said a minute later, grinning, "you know all about it. Shouldn't wonder if you'd had an education. Shouldn't wonder at all. Now me, I'm not educated. But I've lived a long time in the Enchanted and near the Enchanted. I've seen a lot of things I couldn't explain. Maybe you could. But people in the woods don't explain things your way. You take the Indians. I

used to know an old Indian trapper when I was
a boy. He told me lots of stories of the old days.
There was one about a hunter in his tribe. Every
fall he went off hunting by himself the way
they do, and he was young and got kind of lonesome. 'Wish there was somebody to take care
of my camp,' he says out loud one morning as
he was going off, and that very night when he
got back from hunting he found everything in
apple-pie order and supper cooking over a fire.
This went on for some days and then one evening he found a young woman sitting by the fire.
She was big and strong and turned out not to
be much of a talker. She stayed with him all
winter. In the spring when it was time for him
to take his skins and jerked meat back to the village, she said, 'Please don't get married this
summer.' And he didn't. Next fall soon's ever
he'd made camp, there she was and a little boy
too. Little as he was, the boy went hunting
every day with his father and next spring the
young man went back to his village with twice
as many skins and packs of meat as he'd had before. That made him Number One hunter of the
village and the chief naturally wanted him to
marry his daughter. But he wouldn't."

The old man stopped, puffed at his pipe which had gone out, made an absent-minded and ineffectual attempt to relight it and went on with his story, looking rather at the stove than at David.

"Well, next fall there was the woman again with two little boys and, by gosh! the game they killed the winter before was nothing to what they brought in that winter. In the spring it seemed like the chief would force him to marry his daughter, and finally he gave in and they got married. That fall he took his wife with him into the woods and his father and the chief, too. The woman was waiting for him and this time she had his two boys and a girl. But the Indian wife drove her away. And when the men and the two boys were off hunting, the wife was mean to the little girl who helped her around the camp. So one night the three children ran away. In the morning the father found them gone, and there was nothing in the snow but the tracks of three large animals. So he took his tomahawk and put on his snowshoes and followed the tracks for three days until he come to a clearing with four moose browsing in it. Then he struck his tomahawk into a tree and hung his snowshoes

24

on it and went up to the moose and begged them to let him be a moose too. At first they wouldn't listen, but at last he tired them out and they turned him into a moose too.

"When the hunter didn't come back his old father followed the track of his snowshoes till he come to the place where he found his son's snowshoes and tomahawk. However he looked, he could only see that four moose had entered the clearing and that five had left it."

Chip stopped abruptly and turned his stare on his guest.

"What do you think of that?"

"Nice legend."

"What's that?"

"Fairy story."

Chip started to speak but changed his mind and concentrated his attention upon properly re-filling his pipe. Only after he had smoked for a while did he take up the conversation once more. The sardonic friendliness had come back to his voice.

"You'll find yourself in the middle of one of them legends if you don't look out."

For no reason that he could understand, Dave felt one of those sudden shivers go down his spine. The old traditional warning came into his mind. "Someone's walking on my grave," but he asked casually:

"What am I to look out for?"

Chip lowered his voice and gave the dark window a sidelong glance as he answered, almost in a whisper:

"The Enchanted."

Then before Dave could speak the lumberman put a thick forefinger to his lip, commanding silence. He was listening as an animal listens, absorbed and intent, his eyes expressionless, all his other senses subordinated to the one sense of hearing. And in the silence the two men heard a sudden wind stir in the trees outside, rustling and whispering through the crests of the forest and at last brushing against the cabin and passing down over the river to sound almost inaudibly among the trees on the far side.

When all was silent again, Chip relaxed, put his pipe into his pocket, and Dave rose to go. They shook hands again.

"Hope you'll drop in to see me," Dave said.

"I'm not much for visiting," his host repeated. "I never sit down in another man's chair without I begin to remember some chore at home.

But you come back and see me. And if I can help you out any time, let me know."

To Dave's relief the visit had returned to the everyday cordiality of its beginnings. He didn't want to antagonize his nearest neighbor, however crotchety he might be. But somehow they had got off on the wrong foot. It had begun when he asked about the Perdrys.

Standing in the open door, Chip seemed to read his mind.

"Remember what I said. You go slow when it comes to them down the road. There's more to them than meets the eye. Come again soon."

"Goodnight," said Dave and walked off, his lantern casting a small moving light in the immense, almost soundless landscape.

Again he was aware of the forest all about the man-made clearing, and aware of it a little differently this evening. The Enchanted. The name cast its own spell. Mile after mile, the woods lay about him, closing him in, impenetrable and as far as he knew pathless. Not a lighted window, not another lantern broke its darkness; not a human sound broke its silences. Dave found himself walking quietly as though not to disturb some vast sleeper. But *were* the woods sleeping? He had more a feeling of something waiting, of something watching, but there was no return of the wind. Nothing stirred.

"If you are really the Enchanted, make a sign," he challenged the stillness, and the words had scarcely formed in his mind when a star fell over his dark roof, trailing white fire down the sky.

EARLY SUMMER

It was early morning and the fox stood silvered in the dew-silvered grass, looking down at the fields. He saw the horses in the pasture below him. Horses were not altogether strange to him for he was accustomed to the old black horse at the Perdrys'. His bright gaze followed the cow with her new scent and her queerly awkward motions. A rooster crossed from the Chandler shed, and the fox turned his head for an instant. But he was wary of Chip Chandler, even now that there was no longer a dog on the place. It was Chandler who had shot at him

once or twice, and he had smelled Chandler's hands on the traps around which he had walked cautiously in the woods.

There were no chickens at the Perdry house; only the old horse and the many people. Yet the place and the people puzzled and attracted him strangely, and he spent many of his free hours curled up at the edge of the woods watching their comings and goings.

Now he was studying this new neighbor whose arrival brought further complications and possibilities into his life. This man already had a few hens of his own and only the other day had thrown away a head and chicken legs into the bushes. That was unlike Chandler, who had known his chickens so long and so intimately that he never killed them even when they grew too old to lay eggs.

An incautious field mouse stirred in the grass and the fox shifted his attention from the buildings below him to pounce airily and snap the small creature up. Then he returned to his study of Dead River Farm.

There was smoke rising from the kitchen chimney and as it was early morning, the white column rose straight into the air for twenty feet or more, like the trunk of a tree, before spreading out and dissolving in a faint upper breeze. The fox both saw the smoke and smelled it. He felt the lightness and dryness of the air in every pore of his skin, although his brush and thick coat were at the moment damp and heavy on his body.

Then a door slammed and he saw the new man come out. He had already milked, and now he climbed to the roof of the barn by a ladder leaning against the side of the building. Here and there boards had been clewed in place to support his weight, and the old dark shingles had been pried loose and lay about the ground below, like feathers strewing the leaves after a fox has caught and eaten a partridge. It was now time to hoist up the bundles of new shingles and the man was soon at work hammering them in place. His whistle came up the slope to the attentive ears at the edge of the woods. It was a whistle full of uncertainties and pauses, a breathless, rather tuneless affair, punctuated by the uneven tap, tap, tap of the hammer. Sometimes the hammering stopped altogether while the figure hitched itself a little farther along or pulled out a nail driven in at the wrong angle. Once there came a heavy scrape and a crash as a package of shingles slid on a damp stretch of board, eluded the outstretched hand, and cascaded to the ground.

The fox watched the man climb down the ladder, gather the scattered shingles into a basket and climb back to his perch. The inexpert hammering continued, and the fox had nearly decided to skirt down the ditch to take up his morning hunt by the river, when a new sound caught his ear. It was the Perdry surrey and his old acquaintance the black horse. An excitement seized the fox.

He jumped up, whined a little, ran forward a few steps, thought better of it, ran back again and stood, his nostrils testing the air, his bright eyes clouded with bewilderment. He saw the surrey draw to a stop and watched Mr. Perdry get out and tie the horse by one rein to a tree, while the young people emerged from each side, talking and laughing in low voices. The canopy rocked as the plump quick figures jumped down the carriage steps, their hands full of things. The fox was frozen into the statue of a fox. Every nerve strained in attention. There were so many people to watch all at once, but they kept together, led by the older man, tiptoeing up the drive. The older woman and the four girls softly opened the kitchen door and went

in, softly closing it behind them. With a mar-
shaling glance, the older man saw that the three
boys were behind him, and one after another
they ascended the ladder. At a signal, four new
hammers began to tap below and to one side of
the original carpenter.

The fox heard the whistle die away with a
jerk. Then came men's laughter and voices.

"We thought we'd come over and lend a
hand. The girls were picking strawberries yesterday and saw you. Hope you don't mind their
picking in your fields. Well, neighbors ought to
be neighborly. Don't bother to thank us. We
weren't doing anything special today."

A mouse a little farther down the field ran
from one tussock of grass to another, for once
unnoticed by the fox. The voices of the Perdrys
always excited him. He went hungry listening
to them. But now the hammering began again
and there was little talk. The whole barn rang
with a rat, tat, tat and a rat, tat, tat, falling into a
sort of rhythm, which even caught up the first
man's uncertain hammer and taught it its song.
For a while, the parent swallows hung off in the
morning air, flying in arcs above the high broken
window, afraid to enter. But their young were
inside, and after a little, one bolder than the
others shot into the opening and was gone, and

36

soon another followed, and before long they were all flying unconcernedly in and out and in again with transparent insect wings rosetted at the tips of their bills.

The fox relaxed, scratched his ear which had been itching for some time, and trotted off. These things were all interesting, but a fox must eat every day in the week if he can, and he had given a freer rein to his curiosity already than he could well afford. A little water ran down the bottom of the ditch and before long he came upon a frog which began its jump a second too late.

All morning the work on the roof went on, progressing very evenly and well. Papa Perdry introduced the boys, Jasper, Matthew and Peter. For a while, David tried to tell them apart, mostly by their positions, but as they shifted about he gave up calling them by name. They were accustomed to confusing people.

One of them helped him out.

"I'm Matt and I'm the biggest. I'm at least an inch and a half taller than Papa or any of the others. Jasper is the one whose hair curls a little. He's easy to tell. And Pete's the one who isn't Jasper or me. It's easy if you remember."

And they all laughed. Working there with the

sun on his shoulders and the morning light casting his shadow along the roof, Dave felt a curious contentment. There was about the Perdrys a remarkable unity of mood. They never seemed to pull apart as brothers usually do, and Papa Perdry was one of them and yet had a recognized authority which he never needed to stress because it was so willingly acceded to. A sixth sense told the rest when one needed more shingles or nails. They worked all together, talking, often all together, too, but never so that Dave was confused. Only once or twice he was a little startled when they rose as one man and moved to another part of the roof. He had no warning until the hammering ceased as though the four hammers were one, and he found himself in the midst of this sudden stir and settling. Then the hammers and the talk would begin again.

Dave was an only child himself and he had sometimes wondered what it would be like to be one of a large family. Now he thought it would be a very warming thing.

"But I don't think most families are like them," he thought. "Probably it's because they live off by themselves and have to depend on each other for everything. And perhaps that's the way French Canadians are. They must be

French Canadians. No one I ever knew could talk as much as they do, though with them I like it. Wonder where they picked up the name Perdry."

As he turned to sit on the roof and rest his shoulder for a while, he caught a glimpse of Chip Chandler chopping wood at a block beside his shack. At this distance he seemed all of one color, faded hair, tanned skin, old army shirt and corduroy pants tucked into his boots. As Dave watched, Chip leaned over and filled one arm with kindling and stood for a moment obviously looking towards the barn with its crew of workers.

Dave lifted his hand, but there was no response from the distant figure which turned about and stumped into the shack.

"That Chip," laughed Papa Perdry. "He's a very good man."

"Yes, he got rid of that dog of his. We didn't even have to ask," chimed in Matt, or at least Dave thought it was Matt.

"He's a good man," said Jasper.

"But not a waver," said Pete.

"No, not a waver. You've said it, Pete," chuckled Papa Perdry.

"What was wrong with the dog?" asked Dave.

Many a feud has started over a dog, he thought. Perhaps that explains why he's so queer about them.

"Oh, it scared the girls," Papa Perdry explained readily. "You know: ran out barking when they were berrying and things like that. Chip didn't say anything, but just got rid of the dog."

"That was neighborly," said Dave.

"He's a good neighbor," chorused the Perdrys, "only he isn't what you'd call a waver or a visitor."

"He's smart. You can't fool him," said Jasper.

"Ayah, he's smart," they agreed. "He's smart and he holds his tongue."

Certainly there was no bitterness here, Dave thought. But then these people were all part of a big, good-natured family. Chip was a dried-up, crotchety old solitary, mulling over his thoughts with no one for company but the chickens clucking and squabbling about his feet. All he could think about was going slow. "I'd go slow if I was you." To hell with it. Who was helping him now, Chip or the Perdrys?

When the sun was pretty much overhead and their shadows didn't extend beyond their own busy hands, Papa Perdry called a halt.

"Hi, aren't we going to eat?" he demanded. "Seems to me it's getting to be time."

Dave felt a sudden embarrassment. He had so little to offer them in return for their kindness, but they drowned out his apologies in more laughing assurances, as they climbed down to the ground.

"No, you go in first. It's your house," Papa Perdry insisted at the back door and Dave turned the handle and stepped into the kitchen.

He could scarcely recognize the place. His senses of smell, sight and hearing were assailed at the same moment with a delightful heart-warming rightness. He smelled quantities of hot water and soap and a combined woods' smell, with pine needles in it, and the brewing of tea and the fragrance of baking-powder biscuits. His ears heard the stirring of people and suppressed laughter and the triumphant singing of the kettle, and his eyes took in a kitchen flooded with cleanness and sunlight and girls.

Papa Perdry was at his elbow.

"This is Mama Perdry," he said proudly, and a small round woman bustled forward and shook hands with Dave, smiling, and then came the four girls in a knot, giggling and ducking their heads as he had imagined; Anna, Molly,

Sally and Clotilde, as much alike as their brothers and much like their brothers, too. Dave, looking at Mama and Papa Perdry, thought, "They must be cousins. That's why their children are so alike." But he had little time to consider them. Talking and laughing, the girls showed him about the house.

"Are you sure you didn't guess, Mr. Ross? We told Papa and the boys not to let you get off the roof until we were ready. How do you like it? Clotilde blacked the stove and we all tore off the old wallpaper! What a time we've had. Such fun! Are you surprised, Mr. Ross?"

"Call him Dave," said Papa Perdry, who had followed them. "We're too near neighbors to stand on ceremony."

Sometimes an old-fashioned turn of Perdry speech surprised Dave.

"Sure," he said, "call me Dave."

The sense of being in the heart of a family which he had felt on the roof with the men came back to him, but far stronger. It was almost a physical thing, as relaxing as though he had come into some sort of safety which he had never known. He had seen human beings as isolated creatures, facing the surrounding universe, each man and women alone, now carried along on the sunlit current of individual life, now struggling and drowning in its black floods. But there were so many Perdrys, and each was so much a part of the others, that in their midst life seemed fortified by the common will, the common needs, the common affection. Dave did not take time to analyze his feelings. He merely felt them in a glow of well-being.

"How shall I tell you girls apart?" he asked. "I can tell the boys, most of the time anyhow."

Again merriment shook the family.

"It's easy, Dave, it's easy. Mama? You can tell Mama? Then comes Anna. She's the littlest."

The four girls lined up in front of him. They were all dressed in rather old-fashioned dresses of pretty shades of brown, not plain, but with small patterns, stripes or dots or flowers, worn rather long. Their hair was long, too, fastened up in a knot at the backs of their necks, and one of them had pinned some glossy leaves with a small flower or two in her brown hair which, like Jasper's, was a little curly.

Her name was Molly. Clotilde was the tall one, though certainly not very tall, and the others hesitated to name Sally's distinction, but Sally said, blushing and laughing, "I'm the fat one."

Dave protested. Indeed, she wasn't fat, maybe just a little rounder than the others, but they were all of a type, the almost lost type which one sees in old daguerreotypes where young ladies stood beside photographers' stiles while photographers' snow fell softly about them, and they buried their rounded chins in little round muffs and looked out with large eyes, their cheeks painted with two little spots of pink, their lifted plump arms showing their neat plump forms with many buttons down their bodices and a little bustle-like hike to their skirts.

The Perdry girls were a throwback to this earlier type, housewifely, pretty, cheerful little beings. They surrounded him in a bevy to show him what they had done that morning.

The kitchen looked beautiful. There was even a rose-colored oilcloth on the table under the window and a bunch of wild roses and river iris in a white pitcher on it. The living room was even more surprising. Once again, many hands had stripped off the ragged paper down to the white plaster, only a little cracked. The fireplace had been cleaned out and a small fire was burning there. A wreath of princess pine was hung above it, and two pails of freshly cut pine boughs stood in the corners, scenting the room. The parlor table and another from the hall had been joined together with a long white cloth over them and a flat bouquet of bunchberry and partridge-berry leaves and flowers stood in the center. Chairs had been assembled from all over the house to make the necessary ten, and the table already was decked with dishes of butter, pitchers of cream, big bowls of wild strawberries, a frosted cake and a lemon pie with deep meringue.

"I can't believe my eyes," said Dave. In his wildest dreams he had never imagined the room like this, so sunny, so lively, so welcoming. Through the open windows he could see the river flowing below his fields. And the forest on the other side seemed to have receded, driven back by the sunlight. At that moment he could have thanked God for having brought him to this one place in a wide world where he might so easily have gone elsewhere and lived among other neighbors.

But the women were softly hustling the men.

"We've put the old milking bench and a towel and wash bowl and soap outside by the kitchen door. The pitcher has hot water, or it *was* hot. Wash now, and we'll be dishing up. Everything's ready."

45

When the five men trampled in again, the baked beans and hot biscuits were already on the table at one end and a great pot of tea, surrounded by cups and mugs, stood at the other.

They insisted that Dave should take his place at the head of the table and Mama Perdry sat opposite him.

"Will you have tea or milk?" she asked him. "We're all great tea drinkers in our family," and he took tea with them. His plate was piled with baked beans and two or three biscuits.

"It's a pity we've used up the last of the cabbages, or we could have cole slaw. Baked beans don't taste quite right without a little cabbage to go with them."

But Dave found nothing wrong with the meal. Now Dead River Farm had really come alive. He had been only camping in its ruins, and its forlornness irked him all the time, but he had steadfastly insisted upon spending his strength on the land. In the winter he had planned to do something like this. He had thought he'd have time after the firewood was stacked. And now it had been done for him in a morning, as a gesture of friendliness. In a babble of talk and laughter and quick hands, the work had all been done for him.

47

"I'll send to Sears Roebuck's for some shades and window curtains," he said, "and I suppose there ought to be a rug."

But Mama Perdry and the girls all protested together against the rug.

"We're going to cut up the old carpet which was here and take the good parts and put a few rows of braided wool cloth around them—it will only have to be a foot-wide border—and you'll have two or three of the prettiest braided-and-carpet rugs you ever saw. We have just the right rags in the shed."

"You're too kind," exclaimed Dave, overwhelmed.

But they only laughed.

"We have to do *something* to keep so many of us busy. And there's no use your paying out money for things that can be made at home. There's a hanging shelf in your shed chamber, too, and a pretty picture of deer drinking by a waterfall. All it needs is a new glass."

Green and white and brown. It was a real forest room. It had come about without any conscious planning, at least on his part. Dave sat back enjoying everything. Never a talker himself, the continual talk of the Perdrys didn't annoy him. It had a naturalness about it, almost like wind in branches; it ran from one member of the family to another, round and round the table, and he was free to take part in it, or, if he preferred, to listen.

Only once was the unruffled good humor of the meal for a moment disturbed. The windows in the upstairs chambers had been left open and a chair, which may have been already off balance, suddenly fell over, hitting the floor above their heads with a loud and unexpected bang. Instantly, the Perdrys were on their feet amid a great noise of chair legs scraping along the floor, and one of the girls—Anna, probably— swept a plate off the table in her hurried rising. A moment later they were laughing at themselves.

"Mercy, weren't you startled?" they asked Dave. "But no, you never moved. You aren't so silly." And Molly said, "I nearly screamed. Any sudden noise frightens me so."

Later Dave remembered this incident when he was inclined to think that the Perdrys might be part Indian. The Indians, he knew, were supposed to be very superstitious. Living in the deep woods as they always had, moving on a very narrow trail between life and death, they were prone to attribute strange powers to the

49

elements of nature, and their senses were strung tighter than were those of white men. Still, he could not think of them as so volatile as the Perdrys. That quality fitted in more with his ideas about the French, and perhaps this life of theirs at the very edge of the wilderness had developed in them a family timidity. If, as he thought possible, Papa and Mama Perdry were cousins, the trait might very easily have been stressed in their children, as he had read recently in his books on horse breeding that good and bad elements were likely to become emphasized in a closely-related family.

The Perdrys may have been easily startled, but if so, their recovery was also very quick. In less than a minute, they were eating and talking as merrily as ever, as though nothing had happened to alarm them. An hour went by all too quickly and the men sat back smoking their pipes and cigarettes.

"Well, this is something like," said Papa Perdry beaming upon the whole table. "We've always been a little lop-sided in this family. Needed another boy to round us out. I move that we elect Dave as an honorary member of the Perdry clan. Who seconds the motion?"

"I second the motion," said Mama Perdry

good-humoredly, and without waiting to be called upon to vote, the young people shouted "Aye."

"Maybe Dave doesn't want to be an honorary member," said Molly, who sat next to him, more gravely than was usual with a Perdry, but Dave, flushed with pleasure, got up and made a regular after-dinner speech, telling how honored he was to be included, and everyone clapped, and called "Hear! hear!" in a manner at once old-fashioned and a little British—or perhaps Canadian.

Papa Perdry was the first to rise. "While we sit here the sun goes right on traveling. We'd better get back to our shingling if we're to do a good day's work. Will you and the girls wait, Mama, or will you drive back home when you've readied up here?"

"We've still got the upstairs chambers to do, Papa," Mama said. "We'll have the whole house nice for Dave by suppertime. Maybe we'll stay and have a cup of tea ready for you when you're through work. Might as well make a day of it while we're here."

Molly reached out and took a strawberry from those left in the bowl nearest her. "I found that. It's the biggest I ever found! It's for Dave."

She hesitated and Mama Perdry cried out:

"Go on! Give it to him! He won't mind your fingers. A pretty girl's fingers make a berry taste sweeter, don't they, Dave?"

MIDSUMMER

A week of rain at the beginning of July put
off haying at Dead River Farm longer than
Dave had intended. The barn roof was finished
before the rain began—he had done the last of it
by himself—and he felt well enough established
to take a second trip down to the settlements,
from which he returned with a second mare
bought at a horse-breeding farm east of Waterville. Daisy-Belle was a better-tempered and bet-
ter-looking animal than his old Alice, but he did
not feel the confidence in her that he felt in the
veteran. For one thing, she was lacking in char-

53

acter and will, and Alice tyrannized over her as she never troubled to tyrannize over the team. Now, with four large horses grazing at once, the pasture began to look used. If anyone had passed by, he might have guessed that this was a stock farm.

Between the rain and his trip, it was the tenth of July before Dave began to cut his upper meadow. The grass was heavy and coarse with neglect. It would be better next year and he hoped to lay out part of the ground to clover. He was new to the work, although he had read up on the subject and had kept a sharp eye on the haying methods at the farms along the Waterville road. Still, it was lucky that Pat and Patience were old hands at haying. He began on the smallest field and cut only half of it, his eyes continually on the clouds. He was obsessed by the fear of rain, although he had so much hay for his five head of stock that this year he could afford to lose half his crop while learning. Another year it would be different, when he had more horses to winter. He remembered once saying to a farmer, "It must take courage to hay," and the man had answered with a curious, half-bitter, half-humorous twist of his mouth:

"It takes courage to do anything on a farm."

Dave was beginning to understand this: everything was a gamble between man and nature. The raccoons had eaten most of his lettuces and killed several hens. Cutworms were attacking the squashes. If his apples were to be good for anything, he'd have to get to town for more spray, but he couldn't do that until he'd cut his hay. Or ought he to go when half the hay was in? A man on a farm, he could see, had a good many decisions to make, and they had better be wise ones if he were going to have enough to eat on his table.

So Dave rode the mowing machine, reflecting upon his lot, but at the same time exalted by the steady sound of the long grass swishing to its fall in a green slanting wave behind him. He kept his eyes out for rocks, afraid of hurting the blade. The team obeyed quickly. Their ponderous motion would halt on half a step. And they were willing. Dave thanked goodness that he didn't have to shout and bully them. So far as he could see, they were truly matched and neither one hung back and left the harder work to the other.

All the first night of his haying, Dave kept waking, listening for rain. He got up early. The day was beautiful, with dew on the grass. He let it dry a little as he did his chores and then took Pat out with the light rake. By noon, he had the half field tidily arranged in long windrows. He was very proud of them, although there was no one to see them but the eagle which every afternoon came, slowly circling out of the Enchanted to examine the open lands, and then drifted off up the river. Chip Chandler, too, kept his eye on things, but from a distance. For nearly an hour in the late afternoon, Dave saw him comfortably seated on his doorstep, smoking his pipe while he watched Dave raking his windrows into mows. There was no sign of the Perdrys. They had not passed again in the surrey going to the Forks, nine miles away, and none of the girls had been berrying at the edge of the woods.

The sun went down among light clouds and Dave was worried for his first hay. That evening after supper he went over to see Chandler who greeted him cordially.

"Looks nice to see haying going on again," he remarked, making an opening which Dave seized immediately.

"I'm planning to get it in tomorrow morning," he said. "I'm afraid it may rain. I was wondering if you could come over and make the load while I pitch." He hesitated, knowing that he was treading now on dangerous ground. "I'd be glad to fix things up with you," he finished a little vaguely.

Chip did not answer immediately. The two men were sitting side by side on the shack steps and their pipes more or less kept off the mosquitoes which came humming out of the dusk. Above the forest, the evening sky was almost white, but not white enough to quite dim the brilliance of the planet quivering low over the tree tops like a single drop of dew.

"You're in too much of a hurry," Chip said at last. "I told you a while back to go slow. If you put your hay in tomorrow morning, it'll ferment and end by burning your barn down. You got to wait until afternoon and maybe until next day."

"But it looks like rain," Dave said.

"Maybe it'll rain and maybe it won't. There's been wet hay before this. One rain don't hurt it too much. For that matter, there's been spoiled hay, too, for as far back as I can remember. You just burn it where it lies. But that's better than having your barn go and maybe them big horses, too, some night."

Dave sat letting this sink in. He couldn't bear to think of his work being wasted—of the team's, too—of his time being wasted, of his pride in the field, as well. But slowly he accepted the discipline of patience. He could roof a barn, maybe, at his own speed because that had to do with man-made things, but nature could not be hurried. He would have to let her take her own time. Dimly he saw that he had chosen to serve a dark force, fruitful but capricious, giving with one hand and suddenly, harshly, withholding with the other.

"Of course I'll help you," Chip broke the silence again. "Glad to." He disposed of the last clause of Dave's speech succinctly. "Maybe some day in the fall I'll ask for the loan of your team to bring in my wood."

They sat looking ahead of them. A whippoorwill was calling from a long way off, and now they heard the river which they usually did not notice because it was always there.

"Likely we can get it in by afternoon if the sun shines good," Chip comforted Dave's impatience. "What do you think of the Perdrys?"

"They seem good neighbors," Dave said cautiously, but even this answer amused Chip.

"I'll say they're good," he wheezed. "They near took over your place, didn't they? I thought you might go flying off with them and I'd never see you again. Been down to see them yet?"

"Yes," said Dave a little stiffly. "I've called two or three times. They have been very kind."

"Oh, they're all good-hearted. That I will say for them. And those black-eyed girls are a pretty sight. Four of them, ain't they? Did you see any garden planted when you was there?"

"Why, no," said Dave.

"Any chickens, any pig?"

"No, they said they weren't much as farmers."

"Hadn't cut any hay for that old horse?"

"No. They'd burned over the lower field."

"That's for blueberries. Makes them grow better."

"The Indians used to do that, didn't they?"

There was a pause. Dave felt that there was something he should guess for himself. The old lumberman was giving him the clues, but he must find the answer for himself, if he were to find it at all.

"Mr. Perdry and the boys probably trap and hunt a little, too," he said tentatively. But Chip grunted.

"No. They live mostly on tea and bread and what berries the girls pick. Ever since they come here in April."

Of all the things which Chip had said this

surprised Dave most. The Perdry house was old and worn, in need of paint, its furnishings clean but shabby. He had taken it for granted that they had lived there for years and years and that the children had been born there.

"I thought they were local people!"

Again came that queer chuckle.

"I guess you could call them local."

Dave sat silent. There was something very queer about the Perdrys. Or was it about Chip? He thought of the big family down the road gathered about the lamp, all turning to welcome him. It was Molly who had opened the door that first time he knocked. Of all the young people, he could recognize her most easily because of her pretty curly hair and because she tucked partridge-berry leaves into it at the back. None of the other girls did that. And though they all seemed glad to see him, Molly seemed gladdest. Of course they were a happy-go-lucky lot, living from hand to mouth, on credit for all he knew, but he liked them. Whenever he was with them, he felt that flow of family feeling, of group co-operation which he had noticed the first day.

And here in the dark with a small, thin moon hanging high over the pine tops at the edge of the Dead River, with Chip beside him, everything seemed strained and double-edged, suspicious and solitary. He remembered the lumberman's tales of the Enchanted behind them, of the voices which cried for help, of the music where there were no instruments, of the bewitched buck which changed into a bear. And according to Chip, the queer things which the Enchanted could do went right on happening.

"He's gone a little crazy living by himself," Dave thought. "That's it. And nobody knows it."

But who was there to know it? Only the Perdrys, who spoke of him tolerantly, but avoided his shack. Only Dave himself, to whom everything was strange. He had taken the older man for granted as forest-hardened and shrewd. When he said, "Go slow," Dave had felt a warning and had been inclined to obey it. He had held back a little, he scarcely knew from what.

But now he saw that Chip was crazy, or "cracked," as people say. His head was ringing with queer fancies. Probably he thought Dave had come to this forgotten spot because he had committed a forgery. Probably he had a whole story made up about him. If anyone should ever come to see Chip, he'd sit, nodding down at Dead River Farm:

"I guess the young fellow who's taken the old place came here for his country's good. I make out he used to be a bank clerk or whatever they call them. Made an extra good thing out of it, if you ask me."

When you dealt with the imaginings of a crazy man, any story was possible.

"I'd better be going," said Dave. "Thank you about the hay. I'll be seeing you tomorrow."

"What's your hurry?" Chip called after him. "If you want to go calling some more, the Perdrys are away. There hasn't been a light in their windows for three nights now."

"Thanks," said Dave. He had already reached the road. He had had no intention of going to see the Perdrys, but Chip's words put the idea into his mind. He was disturbed, almost angry, although he knew that Chandler was not to be blamed if he had found the weight of the all-encompassing wilderness more than he could bear. Would he, himself, ever go back into the Enchanted, Dave wondered. Would he ever see its almost unknown ponds and mountains, its vast groves, and its streams which disappeared and were lost to sight? Possibly, some day. But not for long enough to go crazy, he hoped.

He found himself striding past his own dark

house, and Patience, hearing his footfall, whinnied once from the pasture. In that immense loneliness he felt grateful for even an animal's greeting. He'd better get a dog. Funny, there wasn't a dog in the settlement, if you could call three houses in a hole in the wilderness a settlement. He heard an owl hoot somewhere in no-man's-land and another answer from far off, mates hunting on silent wing, miles apart, stopping to signal to one another under the stars.

He passed his own last wall. Here the really cultivated land ended. The ruts dipped down a little through a fringe of alders and birches; then came open land, half grown over with clumps of bushes. He heard rabbits running past. It was a great place for rabbits and birds. Then the road turned a little. There was a light in the Perdrys' windows.

Somehow the fact was a great relief to Dave.

"The crazy old liar," he thought and then he forgot about Chip. As his feet sounded across the old boards of the verandah, the door opened and he heard someone say in the doorway:

"Hello, Dave, I was hoping you'd come over." He knew who it must be.

"Molly?" he asked low, and she said:

"Yes, it's Molly," holding out her hand.

He took it and drew her out to the verandah. She came willingly enough, closing the door behind her with her left hand.

"The mosquitoes," she said.

They were alone in the darkness of the porch. It was the first time that he had ever been with her except in the presence of the whole family.

"Molly," he repeated.

He could hear her quickened breathing from somewhere at about the level of his heart. It seemed very natural to open his arms and draw her close. She nestled against him, making faint sounds of endearment, scarcely words at all, full of warm tenderness. Through the cracks of the door and the windows, the good-humored sound of the family talk came out around them. They were enveloped in it even here, and yet it seemed not to intrude upon their privacy, but to sustain it.

There was not very much which had to be said. Once Dave murmured, "I love you," and later he said, "I hope we can get married soon." As for Molly, she did not actually say anything at all. She merely clung to him, and her answering kisses said, "I love you," and said, "Of course we'll be married soon," without any need for words.

After a while, one of the boys opened the door. "Hi, Molly!" he shouted into the darkness.

"I'm here, Matt," answered Molly, speaking over her shoulder without irritation.

"Oh, excuse me!" exclaimed Matt. "We thought maybe you'd gone off," and he closed the door again. From the verandah the two could hear the burst of kindly laughter and talk which greeted some announcement.

"We'd better go in and tell them," said Dave.

There was only one lamp in the room, but it gave a good deal of light. Dave saw the faces turning to him and they were all, Papa's and Mama's, the boys' and girls', almost as loving as Molly's own. The whole family swept about him, welcoming him in.

"Molly and I are going to be married," he said and they cried:

"How lovely! How wonderful! We're *so* glad," and Papa Perdry shook his hand over and over and Mama Perdry and the girls kissed him and the boys clapped him on the shoulder. He was almost buried under their kindness. But he liked it, and all the time he kept his left arm snugly about Molly's waist, and she kept her left hand over his, in a tender, confiding gesture which he found touching.

"We're going to be married soon," he boasted, and still there were only exclamations of pleasure. It seeemed not to occur to anyone to say, "Go slow"—why did that phrase ring through his head?—no one suggested any cause for delay. It was all happening so rapidly. He was a little bewildered.

"I suppose Molly will have to get ready."

"Oh, she has another dress," Mama Perdry said. That seemed to settle it.

Dave was a little taken aback. He had vague memories of hearing about the weeks necessary to prepare for weddings, and the invitations to be sent out and Lord knows what all. This simplicity seemed strange, attractive, but a little terrifying in its starkness. The words "poor white" flashed across his mind. Were the Perdrys poor white? But no, poor white suggested something run-down and even perverted. The atmosphere here was one of health and sanity and a kind of natural balance. Papa Perdry was gazing upon him with satisfaction.

"Mama and I have said a hundred times that we ought to have four boys, and now you come along, Dave, and just fill up the family."

It was as though he were marrying all the Perdrys, of course Molly in particular, but still all of them. They weren't happy just for Molly's sake, but for their own, and their affection could widen that much more to take him in.

Jasper went out to the well and brought in a bucket with a dozen bottles of root beer, ginger ale, orangeade and lemonade in it, which the boys had left hanging just above the cold underground water.

"Must have known what was going to happen, Dave," he announced with a grin. "Mama, haven't we some old doughnuts?"

Mama Perdry hurried off, returning with a heaping plate of sugar cookies, a little dry but good, and the girls brought glasses, and Papa Perdry opened the bottles and each named his choice, beginning with Molly and Dave.

Papa Perdry proposed the first toast:

"To Dave, our new son!" and everyone jumped to his feet to drink, and Dave, glancing at Mama Perdry, felt a queer pang in his heart at seeing the tears of joy glistening in her kind dark eyes.

His own father and mother weren't a bit like this. They held everything off and looked at it from a distance, turning it over and over in their minds to see what might be wrong with it. They had always been self-sufficient, not much needing even one son. There would be no tears of joy in his mother's eyes when she greeted a daughter-in-law, any daughter-in-law. But his parents were far off in Florida, living on savings, and raising a few chickens to help the savings stretch. It would be a long day before they saw Molly, tears or no tears.

Before Dave left that evening, it was arranged that they would be married as soon as he could get the license. He could scarcely tear himself away from the warmth and kindness of the room to go out into the dark and solitary night walled in and brooded over by the high tree tops of the Enchanted. Every time he started to get up, loving hands pushed him back into his chair, and loving voices cried out to him to stay. In all this affection and good cheer there was nothing false. It rose spontaneously from the heart, and Molly's hand lay simply and happily in his, and all evening her eyes rested on him in open pride and contentment.

The crazy old alarm clock in the kitchen rang twelve before Dave could bring himself at last to go. He kissed Molly before them all. It seemed natural to let her people share in the love which was between them; there was no need for whispers at the door and quick kisses in the darkness of a hallway.

"Well," said Matt, "we didn't guess this

morning what we were coming back to, did we, Molly?"

As Dave strode down the crazy road in the starlight, Matt's words recurred to him. So they *had* been away. At least Chip hadn't lied about that.

LATE SUMMER

As Dave drove out of the woods, he honked vigorously and Chip came hurrying from his door, waving a torn dishcloth and grinning. Dave stopped his car and Chip shook hands with Molly.

"Congratulations, Molly. And I better congratulate the groom. I ought to have said that first, I guess. I ain't much used to this marrying business. Ain't ever gone through it myself."

He looked at them both shrewdly, his old eyes amused and good-natured. Suddenly he slapped his thigh.

"Don't it beat the Dutch!" and he began to laugh. "Say, Molly, did you know how to fill all them things out—name, age and everything?"

"Of course," said Molly. "I asked Mama and wrote what she said: 'Molly Perdry, born June 6th, 1933, Dead River, the Enchanted.' "

Chip whistled admiringly. "Don't women beat the Dutch!" he repeated and turned towards Dave. "And I suppose you wrote your piece. And then you both said, 'I will,' and everyone kissed the bride."

"No," said Dave. "I did any kissing that was to be done. But the clerk at the registry office said Molly was the prettiest bride he'd seen for a coon's age."

Dave that morning had been a little embarrassed to find that Molly was getting married in one of her brown sprigged dresses. Only her small red shoes had a holiday look, but even they were old-fashioned, like the way she did up her hair. She had a new-picked bunch of partridge-berries pinned at the back of her neck, as usual. She certainly was a pretty sight, and fresh as a flower, but he was afraid she'd be stared at in town.

Once he had her on the street she was stared at all right, but he could tell it was with admiration. He hadn't considered what people would think about Molly when he kissed her on the porch of her house the other evening, but he wasn't sorry to find that she could hold her own with any of the village girls. He needn't be on the defensive when he took his wife to town. Dave could see that.

"And now I suppose you two are setting off on a honeymoon," Chip went on benignly.

"Just for a few days. We thought we'd go camping a little."

"That's the idea," said Chip. "You'll find Molly's a good little guide. I guess you won't go in very deep. Well, I'll be glad to keep an eye on the stock for you. Stay as long as you like. I'll see that you find everything like you left it, when you come back."

"Thanks," said Dave, really grateful. He hadn't been sure just how Chip would take his marriage. "But I guess the boys can do that. The horses will look after themselves. It's just the one cow to milk and the chickens to feed and water."

Chip turned to Molly.

"You tell your husband he'd better let me do the milking. No Perdry in this world would remember two days running that a cow has to be milked. Ain't that so, Molly?"

"Yes, Dave," she said, "you'd better leave it to

73

Mr. Chandler. Like as not the boys would go off and forget all about the cow."

"Then I'll be much obliged to you," said Dave. "And there's a new mare coming today or tomorrow. She's been paid for, but would you have the men put her in the lower pasture with the others? I'm going to leave them down there while we're gone so they can drink whenever they've a mind to."

Their camping equipment was very simple: a few blankets wrapped in heavy oilcloth which they would lay on the ground; a knapsack of provisions; a frying pan and an old blue coffee pot, and they were ready. But before they started off, Chip tapped at their door.

"I brought you a wedding gift," he said to Dave, handing him a paper in which they found three very beautiful trout flies carefully wrapped. "They might come in handy. I made them myself."

He looked pleased at Dave's praise, and went off immediately.

"You'd better be getting started if you're going," he called back from the road. "I'll drop in, Molly, and tell your family everything's all right so far, and that Dave ain't et you."

And grinning, the old man went off.

"He's nice," said Molly softly. "Has he ever told you about us?"

"What do you mean?" asked Dave, surprised. But Molly only smiled.

"Please don't ask him questions," she said, in a voice which sounded only faintly troubled, and Dave promised. He had no desire to ask anyone questions about his wife or her family at the time.

Dave had been too busy in these busy weeks ever to go into the forest, although he had been always aware of it, like something waiting there before his eyes across the river and walling in his sunlit fields. The shadow of the Enchanted lay across everything he did. Dawn was caught in the darkness of its high pines and held back a little from the clearing, and night came earlier because of the forest. Now as he was at last about to enter into its shadow Dave felt a curious uneasiness, a brush of that feeling which must sweep over trapped things at the moment when the trap snaps to upon them. But the discomfort was gone almost as quickly as it had come.

As Dave followed Molly along the faint trail, he was aware of the smell of the woods all about him. After a little, they came to a clearing overgrown with sumacs, where he could see still the ruins of foundations.

"It's a good place," said Molly. "There used to be a lumber camp here. There's even an old apple tree and someone planted lilacs. The buds come very early because they're out of the wind."

"And you come here to gather lilacs in the spring?" Dave asked.

"Yes, the buds," she said.

They walked on, again in the broken darkness of the forest, Dave's feet crackling among the fallen twigs. Molly, walking ahead, moved lightly and silently, the pack of blankets fastened by a strap across her shoulders. Her sleek head turned from side to side, seeing everything and hearing everything. Sometimes she looked over her shoulder to catch Dave's eye with loving trustfulness and then she would go lightly forward again, intent on the forest, with an attitude at once fearful and at ease.

After nearly an hour, he began to hear the waterfall. She had heard it for a long time, but had not spoken. The sound tumbled and beat and sang with a hundred liquid and musical notes, giving the waiting forest a voice at last, more than the faint sigh of the upper branches, or the passing sound of footfalls. Before long

they could see the stream, like hot silver pouring between black rocks. They made their camp at the head of the falls. A pine tree shaded them, its roots getting their hardy living from the cracks and crannies of the stone. From their place they were too nearly above the falls to see more than the fan of spray which leaped upwards into the light, but they looked instead into the black pool sixty feet below them into which the water fell. It lay between sheer black walls wet with spray and topped by tall, thin pines. For a little the stream seemed to lie dark and quiet and then it rounded into silver once more, straining forward to a second, shorter falls whose continual sweet chidings answered the outcry of the great falls beside which they had spread their possessions.

The light was already deepening into the late afternoon and with an urgency he could scarcely have explained Dave hurried to get their things settled before the darkness came. In everything Molly helped him. They unrolled their blankets and spread them on a bed of spruce boughs which he cut; next he hung their frying pan and pot on two nails driven into the trunk of the pine; then together they built an outdoor fireplace of loose rocks; placed their tins in a neat and convenient row near at hand, and hung up the packsack with the more valuable food from a branch as high as possible above the ground.

"Now," said Molly, "we'll find something to eat before it's dark."

"But we've a lot of stuff here," said Dave, gesturing towards the tins.

"Something good," said Molly. "Come along, Dave. It scares me to be alone."

He knew what she meant. Although they had barely entered into the fringes of the great forest, it seemed immense and profoundly non-human. It was heavy with power, with a will which had nothing to do with man, and made no compromise with him as the clearings did. Here the scale between man and nature was tipped altogether on the side of nature, and a nature inscrutable and secret. Dave began to understand Chip and his stories better here than he had understood them that first evening sitting on the kitchen chair by the lumberman's stove.

"Is this the Enchanted Stream?" he asked Molly, and she nodded her head.

"Where does it disappear underground?"

She turned and said softly, "Oh, that is a long way from here. Between Upper and Lower En-

79

chanted Ponds. I have never been so far. But my grandfather used to go as far as Lower Pond."

"Lumbering?" Dave asked. Molly's dark trustful eyes rested on his.

"No. He wasn't a lumberman. Just—well, camping. Like us."

Voices naturally were lower in the woods. Somehow it seemed wiser not to call too much attention to oneself. Molly moved very softly indeed and spoke very softly here. She had led them away from the trail and was searching here and there with quick, gentle motions. Then all at once she uttered a faint exclamation of pleasure, calling Dave to look. She had found a large puffball, nearly the size of her head, shaped like a round loaf of bread.

"What's that?" Dave asked.

"Wait until I fry it for you for supper tonight," Molly murmured. "It's good, oh, so good. I haven't seen one for weeks."

On the way back she found a place where the ground was thick with partridge berries, and these she gathered, leaves and all, into her skirt.

"They taste fresh and clean," she said. "Dave, you have no idea."

"Tomorrow, I'm going to try to catch us some trout with Chip's flies," he promised, and she smiled but said nothing.

They built their fire above the waterfall early, while it was still light, and he found the sliced puffball nearly as good as she had promised. He boiled coffee, which they drank without cream or sugar, and he ate a piece of jelly roll which he had bought in town, but she preferred the berries picked in the woods.

After supper in the late dusk she knelt by the edge of the hurrying stream and washed the camp dishes.

"Don't go away, Dave," she said.

Dave tried to take the dishes. "You might slip." But at that she only laughed.

"I won't slip," she protested. "I'm not afraid of falling in. It's just that I don't like to be alone, ever."

He felt the forest pressing in and down upon them, the unbreakable solitude.

"Now we have each other," he said helping her to her feet when she had finished. He had expected that they would sit by the fire as it died low and talk, talk about the past when they had not known each other, and about the future together which lay ahead for them, but in a few minutes she had fallen asleep with her head against his shoulder.

On the second morning he woke up very early. The sun had not risen, but it would be a fine day, and the trees seemed more absent-minded, as though the forest had its own affairs to attend to, and for a time, at least, had ceased to study the human beings who had entered its precincts. The very trunks seemed to have drawn away from the river a little, and were no longer breathlessly crowding upon the small human encampment there at the edge of the rock.

Although he had lived so long alone, Dave found it perfectly natural to see Molly asleep beside him. He looked at her, careful not to wake her. He wanted to give her things, but he could think of nothing she seemed to want. She was singularly free from the vanities and ambitions of most girls. Neither for herself nor for the house did she appear to have any desires at all.

But his tenderness for her prompted him to some sort of assertive action, and rising quietly, he took his rod and Chip's flies and went as noiselessly as he could down the trail which ultimately led below the second falls where he hoped there might be trout. A string of trout for breakfast, fresh from the water, would surprise and please her, he thought.

He, too, could support them in the wilderness.

For nearly an hour he fished, while the pallid

light of the false dawn turned to true dawn, and as he had thought, there were plenty of trout.

He had four on the bank and was thinking of going back when he began to hear sounds of distress above the rush of the stream. At first he paid little attention to them, but as the noise continued, he grew worried, wondering what sort of animal or bird could be uttering these cries, and hoping that Molly would not be frightened.

As he thought of Molly and her timidity, he began to hurry up the steep path, stumbling over the roots and crashing through the underbrush like a bear. He was hot and out of breath when he reached their camping place. Above his hurry, he had heard the cries growing louder, but as he pushed past the pine there was no sound except the sound of the waterfall, and then, Molly threw herself into his arms, sobbing hysterically.

"Oh, Dave, Dave, Dave," she kept saying through her sobs. "I was so frightened. Don't leave me alone. Dave, how *could* you? All alone?"

Dave felt guilty. At dawn it had seemed natural and pleasant to go fishing, but as he felt her trembling shake his body and his cheek grow wet with her tears, he thought that he had been a fool to leave her.

After a while she became quieter and lay exhausted in his arms.

"I'm so foolish," she whispered. "Please don't be mad at me, Dave. I'll try to be more sensible. But I'm so used to having the family all around me. I've never been alone. I thought I should die if you didn't come soon."

Later, when he showed her the trout, which even in his anxiety he had managed to bring with him, she looked sad.

"Poor things," she said.

Dave felt that it was time to assert a more rational attitude.

"They're only fish," he replied briskly, taking out his hunting knife to clean them for a breakfast now overdue. "Can you start up the fire, Molly, while I get them ready?"

For a moment longer Molly stood gazing at the fish. Her soft brown hair hung round her shoulders. She wore a straight-cut flannelette nightgown like a robe and her feet were bare. The early sunlight fell palely on her troubled face.

"I don't know how to say it," she said in that low voice of hers. "Life is all that any of us really has. And when anything loses, it, I feel sad."

She looked like a saint and talked like a saint. Dave hardened himself against her.

"You're a little goose," he said. "Now get dressed while I clean them. No, I'm just going to the edge of the stream," and turning his back on her, he walked over to the water and sitting on his heels, got the trout ready for the pan.

Later, Molly ate her fish under his eye, and said it was good. She was dutiful and tried to please him, but he saw that she ate fast to get the irksome task over.

"There's nothing so delicious as trout just out of the water," he declared, savoring each mouthful, and she quickly agreed. "Yes, Dave, and today I shall find coral mushrooms for us."

The weather held good and they went exploring up the steam. Molly brought a dishcloth in which to tie up the things she might find for their dinner. She seemed to have a sixth sense for berries and mushrooms. Once they came upon a slash where the lumbermen had worked not too many years before, and here Molly was beside herself with delight over the raspberries and early blackberries she found. She ran from bush to bush, her quick fingers flying, exclaiming with pleasure and continually looking about with soft timid eyes to make sure that Dave was

near her. Her dependence upon him touched
him deeply. She was like a child, like a dove
that nestled in his bosom, looking to him for
defense against the world. He had never known
what it was before to have another person look
to him for safety as well as for love; in fact, no
one before had looked to him for anything much
except to do as he was told.

Their explorings ended at a fir tree beside
the stream, where Dave saw two boots hanging
from a branch.

"For heaven's sake!" he exclaimed, stopping
in his tracks. "What are those old boots doing
there?"

Molly leaned against him.

"It's the custom with the lumbermen," she
said softly. "They hang a man's boots above the
head of his grave. I've seen them on the Dead
River where the men have been drowned during the spring drives."

She made a motion as though to go on again,
but Dave felt a saddened curiosity and, holding her hand, went nearer the spot. The old
boots had been securely nailed to the bough.
They were hardened by exposure to something
like metal or bark, but still they bore the im-
print of their wearer, the bulges which once had

been shaped by the pressure of flesh and bone, the scuffed places in the leather, the creases, and the thinning of the warped soles which had been worn off by the friction of thousands of steps along the floor of this forest where they now stood.

The wearer had been a tall man; at least his boots were large boots. Dave wondered what his name had been and as he wondered, he glanced at Molly and saw that her eyes were intent on something beyond and below the boots which he had not noticed. It was a flat gray strip of board on which had been printed in black paint not unskillfully:

"The many friends of Judson Pratt will mourn his death. He was lost December 27th, 1942, near Lower Enchanted Pond, and his body was found on April 4th, 1943, at this spot."

Molly said, "He heard a Voice."
"You know about what happened?"
"Everyone knows," Molly went on. "They sing a song about him. He heard a Voice calling him which none of the others heard. He got away from them and the snow began to fall and they couldn't follow his tracks. Some people say he

went crazy. But it was the Voice of the Enchanted. It has happened before."

She spoke soberly, and in quite a matter-of-fact tone, and Dave knew that it was no more use to argue with her than with Chip Chandler, although she was outwardly so yielding. Here in the watchful shadow of the trees by the swift, almost silent flow of the stream, he had less impulse to discuss the forest than he had felt earlier in the summer among the fields. He was sure that it was only his fancy, but here there seemed to be a vast listening. It was more than the listening of the animals and birds which quite possibly were aware of them, holding themselves motionless and alert whether from curiosity or fear, unseen somewhere in the shadows. Their animal listening was only a small part of the general listening of the woods, an attention at once impersonal and vague and yet curiously focused upon the two humans and every motion which they made and the sound of their voices.

Mostly their few days at the waterfall passed without much outward incident. One day it rained, and they rigged up a shelter of boughs over their bed and were damp and merry. Another day, in the raspberry slash, Molly met a fox when she had wandered a little away from

Dave and came running back to him, startled
and out of breath.

"Molly!" he protested, annoyed and yet
touched by her timidity. "You act like a child.
Why, a fox couldn't hurt you any more than a
kitten."

"I know, Dave," she admitted penitently. "I'll
try to remember. I'm a young lady now. I don't
have to be afraid of foxes. I'm Mrs. Molly Perdry Ross. Now kiss me and I'll fill my basket
again. I spilled them, I was so startled. But don't
you leave that stump, will you, Dave? I want to
know just where you are."

The last day or two they scarcely left their
camping site. It was the prettiest place they had
found and most theirs. The openness of the
stream let in the light, and their possessions gave
the spot an air of permanence. This little place
they had made their own. The stream seemed
to sing its continual braided song especially for
them, and the big pine tree sheltered them as
though it liked them. They sat for many hours
between its curving roots, their backs to its wide
trunk, looking out at the water flowing by, always new water, and new ripples of light, yet
always essentially the same stream catching the
sunlight in the same net of motion. They talked

sometimes and sometimes they merely sat close together feeling the bond between them tightening in the silence.

It was while they sat talking together on one of these last days that Dave happened to ask Molly if she had ever read some book or other and she surprised him by saying simply:

"No. There weren't any books at the house when we came. I've never read a book."

For a moment he thought, "She's illiterate!" with a shock of distaste. Then he remembered that she had made out the slip for her marriage license. He said:

"You read the papers, don't you, the funnies?"

She sometimes seemed so simple that he thought of her as interested in childish things, but this was always a mistake. She was clear as glass, very direct, but she was adult.

"I hate the funnies," she said. "Don't you? But sometimes there are poems and some of the editorials are nice. I don't understand about government and I've never seen anyone from Europe, except some Finns from the valley, but once in a while the editorials are about the crops or about people or what is right and what is wrong, and I like those."

"Does your father read them to you?" Dave

insisted. But she had no idea of the anxiety which prompted the question.

"Sometimes, but mostly I read them myself." She began to laugh in her low voice. "Usually it's when I'm filling the lamp on a newspaper that's weeks old, or wrapping something up, and I catch just a word or two and get so interested I sit right down to read the rest while the work waits."

The last days of their honeymoon were perhaps the happiest, and yet for each of them there was an element of increasing restlessness which intruded upon their content. Dave wanted to get back to the farm to make sure that everything was all right there. A week was a long time to be away in summer, especially during this first summer. And Molly hungered for her family and the crowded room and the talk and kindness and banter about her. If only Dave could have been ten people at once, she would have been perfectly happy, but life in a large and congenial household had made her very vulnerable to loneliness. She secretly wished that Dave would come and live with the Perdrys, or ask her family to live with him, but she realized that neither of these arrangements would suit him, and she never spoke of them.

At Dead River Farm, however, she would be only a short distance from home, and she would be dropping in to see her people, and they would be coming in to see her all day long. She could scarcely wait to be back, and yet these hours alone with Dave were very sweet, the sweetest she had ever known. She wanted to learn to live in Dave's way.

"It will be nice to be back at the farm," Dave said, and Molly said, "It will be lovely." And he thought of the fields he had cleared and the shine of the new shingles in the morning sunlight, and the broad backs of the horses, and the plowing he meant to begin, and she thought of the joy of having all her people about her again, of feeling submerged in the common will and the common happiness once more.

And over them both the big pine stretched out its branches as though saying to the forest, "These are my guests. Let them alone. They have come to me for protection in their love," and the Enchanted stood silent, a little withdrawn from them, but listening and waiting, darkening into night long before the light had left the sky overhead, long before the first stars appeared.

"N o," said Mama Perdry, her quick hands flying over the great basket of late blackberries and thimbleberries beside her on the porch, selecting the good ones for the small basket on her lap, "no, I think Molly will make a very good wife."

"But they are so different," said Papa Perdry. "Dave's upbringing hasn't been at all like hers."

The boys were away, helping to put up an addition to the garage at the Forks. They were good carpenters, but could only be hired when Grayson Hobbs at the grocery refused the family further credit, and then they would work for the few necessary days and be gone. They had a reputation for never finishing a job, but while they worked, they worked well, and people were glad to get whatever help they could. Mama and the girls were more to be counted on in building up the family exchequer. From the day the first strawberry ripened against its reddening leaves until the repeated frosts rotted the big wild cranberries which lay hidden in the moss, the Perdry women had picked berries for their own table and for Hobbs at the Forks, who paid them as little as he dared and that, of course, only in credit. But as he carried almost everything they needed, thread and nails, overalls, gingham and string as well as groceries, they did not mind. The whole family was very unworldly. If the women hadn't enjoyed berry-picking, they probably would never have done it in the first place.

Now Anna, Sally and Clotilde sat along the unrailed porch, picking over berries like their mother, while Mama and Papa Perdry sat on the steps in the sun, Mama at work and Papa with his pipe, idly watching the smoke as it floated off on the breeze.

Mama's fingers were stained, and so were her

lips, for all the family continually ate the very ripest berries as they worked, and Mama Perdry from time to time put one into Papa's mouth, when he took out his pipe for a moment to tap or refill it.

Sally said, "Molly's changed. When she picks with us now, she just doesn't come along with the crowd the way we all do. She sees berries she wants in the other direction and goes away from us."

"And she doesn't come to see us as often as she did when she first came back," Clotilde added.

"Those are good signs," said Mama. "It is very hard for her, but she is trying to learn to do things in Dave's way. If she can only keep on trying, if nothing happens until spring when her baby is born, it will all be easier for her, and they will be all right."

"Are you sure?" Papa Perdry asked. "I don't know that we have been wise. I feel sad at the thought of leaving her behind. But soon we must be going. I am getting restless. The leaves are beginning to turn—have you noticed? And our young people must meet others of their own age. We have to think of them as well as of Molly."

Mama Perdry popped a large thimbleberry

into her mouth and looked off towards the woods across their grown-over field which was beginning to yellow. The unmowed grass was coarse and pale and filled with goldenrod tufts and plumes already going by. There was an incessant motion of small birds among the alders, and the light had changed. The sun was no longer overhead but lay farther to the south, and that fact changed all the accustomed shadows.

Mama put the filled box to one side and picked up an empty one in its place. She sighed deeply.

"It will be good for her to be alone with Dave," she said. "The best thing we can do for her will be to go soon."

"But she will be so frightened left to herself," said Papa. "I don't like the idea."

"Like it or not, it has to be, Papa," said Mama. "It's their only chance, and as you say, we must think of the others as well."

The girls listened murmuring and looking off across the fields. Their eyes had a new restlessness. Perhaps a marriage in the family had disturbed the perfect equilibrium in which they had all lived until Dave came. Now Molly had a new pink dress; Molly milked the cow. Molly had even ridden on the big mare, Skowhegan

Sue. She was the gentlest of all the horses, in
spite of her big, trampling hoofs and her head
as long as a barrel. The last time the family
dropped in to see her, Molly took them to the
fence to watch her call Sue and feed her an apple, holding her hand flat and not drawing it
back at all.

"And Dave lifts me right on her back and
leads her around by the halter and I like it," she
boasted, her eyes shining with pride.

"But aren't you afraid she'll step on you?"
Mama Perdry asked anxiously, but Molly said
with confidence:

"She can see me perfectly well, Mama. I stand
as high as her shoulder. And I'm taller than the
cow. You ought to see how the cow obeys me
and how quickly I can fill the pail now, almost
as quick as Dave. And I'll show you how the
hens come when I call. It's because I feed them,
you know."

The Perdrys clustered about her, filled with
pride and uneasiness at all her new accomplish-
ments. They had never had a cow nor hens and
their old black horse was so aged and bony and
lackadaisical that he scarcely seemed like a horse
at all. The people who had once lived in their
house had left him behind as they had left the

old stove and the beds. They had somewhere acquired a car and it was in the car that they departed, but because they had had the horse for so many years and were fond of him in a way, they didn't shoot him, but left him behind to starve or freeze in the snow if he lived that long. The Perdrys found the surrey still in the barn and the harness hung on a nail, so one day, all in a mass, they had made out to harness and hitch up the aged creature, and from that time he had taken them to the Forks and back every fortnight, doing most of the driving himself, although Papa Perdry by observation, combined with the method of trial-and-error, learned something of the art of horse management in time.

When Molly had duly shown off the livestock, she led her family into the house, which looked very neat and well-kept, and made them tea and served them gingerbread and sugar cookies. Her great pride was a new alarm clock which she kept on the window sill over the sink.

"At first, I couldn't stay alone more than half an hour, but Dave got me the clock and I learned to wait three-quarters of an hour and then an hour before going out to find him, and now I can stay alone two whole hours! Think of it, Mama!" she exclaimed eagerly, but her eyes had a haunted look which her parents saw with dismay.

"I'd die if I had to be alone for two hours," declared Clotilde flatly.

"So should I," said Anna. "You're wonderful, Molly."

"You're the girl!" said Jasper.

"You bet!" said Matt, and their praise chorused gently about her.

Molly blushed with pride.

"And I have this to help me, too. See, Mama. No, Papa must turn it on. First, twist that button. Is the little light on? Then keep turning the other one very slowly."

A sudden blare of music made them all jump and then laugh.

"My gracious, if it isn't one of those radios! Molly, you certainly are all fixed up," Papa Perdry exclaimed expansively, trying to forget the frightened look he had seen far back in Molly's dark eyes. He didn't look into them again, but kept his glance on her smiling mouth, which was safer. "I suppose you and Dave listen to that in the evenings."

"Yes, sometimes," said Molly, "but I like it especially when I'm here alone. I turn it down low, just to a murmur. I don't listen to what the voices say, but I hear them as though all of you were talking, sometimes men's voices, sometimes women's. If I turn it low enough and don't hear what they say, I can almost think I'm home again. And that helps me wait the two hours. And next week, I'm going to make it two hours and a quarter. It won't be very long, maybe, before I can wait right here until Dave comes in from work. Like other girls."

Mama Perdry went over and put her arms around Molly and kissed her.

"You're a brave girl, Molly," she whispered. "Dave's lucky to have you. If he gets impatient sometimes, you must remember that he can't understand what it's like to have been brought up in a family like ours."

Molly clung to Mama Perdry for a moment. "Oh, he's hardly ever impatient," she answered. "He's wonderful. But it isn't always easy for him, and it isn't easy for me."

Mama Perdry patted Molly on the back and released her.

"People have always to adjust to marriage," she remarked a little drily. "Don't pity yourself, Molly. Nothing's worth having that you don't work for. It will be different in the spring."

"If I can get through the winter," said Molly.

"Of course you'll get through the winter!" Mama declared comfortably.

The Perdrys were very unwilling to leave Molly. It seemed like desertion. The girls helped her wash the tea things and the boys filled the woodboxes, and Papa and Mama sat listening to the radio and laughing at the way people seemed to come popping in and out of Molly's parlor. At last Papa Perdry, glancing out of the window, remarked:

"Looks like Dave's about finished with his plowing for the afternoon. I guess we'd better be skedaddling."

"Won't you stay?" Molly asked, but Papa said:

"No. We were here yesterday. Enough's enough of anything," and the family trailed away, calling back over their shoulders, as they went, to Molly in the door.

One day Dave had to go to the Forks and took Chip along to do his rare shopping. Molly didn't care for town, even such a small, accidental sort of town as the Forks, so she went down the road to spend the morning with her family. Dave and Chip parted in front of Grayson Hobbs' and met in an hour and a half.

Chip's biggest parcel was a burlap sack with a tom cat's head peering out of the top, which was tied firmly about its neck to keep the creature from clawing or getting away.

"The Driscolls were clearing out the extra cat population of their barn afore winter," Chip explained, "and I kind of took a fancy to this young fellow. He's black with a white spot at the tip of his tail, just like a fox's."

The cat stared at Dave from two eyes as green and expressionless as green grapes. Chip kept the bag on his knees as they drove home and the cat sat quiet but tense as though ready to spring the moment the man's hands should be gone from its sides.

"He'll be company for you," said Dave, and the lumberman nodded:

"Yes, if he don't run off or take to frightening Molly."

"I guess Molly's not frightened that easy."

"Molly's real timid," said Chip tolerantly. "In some ways it's what you might 'call a timid family."

The next morning was gray with a look of coming rain in the air and Dave was a little late with his milking. As he came out of the barn door, he saw a very curious sight. Molly was standing in the grass beating at something with her broom. As he hurried up, he saw the new cat crouched down as though about to spring, its ears laid back, glaring at the girl from its green eyes. Apparently, each blow knocked it a little off its balance and before it could recover itself for the leap, another blow followed. The cat did not see Dave, but just as he came up, it appeared to have had enough and turned, slinking off. But the victor was not satisfied with mere victory. Molly, whom Dave had never seen anything but gentle, now blazed with anger. With eyes shining, lips parted and face flushed, she pursued the cat, striking at it again and again until it fled before her.

Then she returned, ruffled and triumphant, to Dave, who was in something of a rage himself by this time.

"The nasty brute," he said. "I'll see that Chip puts it out of the way."

"No," Molly insisted. "I'm not afraid of it. Did you see, Dave? I made it run. I scared it, Dave. If it comes back, I'll beat it again. I'm not afraid of it. I made it run." She leaned the broom against the house and twisted and pinned her hair back into place and gradually her breathing subsided and the color left her face.

All day she kept recurring to the incident.

"I wonder, Dave, if that cat will try to come back," and looking up, he would see her smiling to herself.

It rained hard that day and for two days after and Dave brought in the horses and worked about the house and barn. Alice would have her colt soon and then Dead River Farm could begin to call itself a real stock farm. But the business would require patience, patience for many months and years. It would be a long time before Alice's colt would be ready for the harness; in three or four years Dave hoped that he would have good young stock. He planned to buy a fourth mare before winter and perhaps in the spring he might pick up two or three two-year-olds to hurry things along. He hoped Mr. Jordan, the manager for the lumber people, would be as good as his word about giving him their teams to board for the summer.

Meanwhile he worked indoors with Molly. They painted the floors and woodwork of the upstairs chambers, the hallway and the stairs. They decided on a black strip like a carpet down the center of the steps. When the paint was dry upstairs, Molly made up the bed in the east room and they painted their own bedroom downstairs. With the shades and curtains and the bed made up with the sunrise quilt, the room looked very fine to them both. They planned to begin on the kitchen next, but they woke up to a day of glittering sunshine and of thickets faded to gold by the downpour.

"It doesn't take frost to change the color," said Dave, "but frost is coming, I must nail those battens down along the cracks of the barn. I don't see any reason for the horses to stand in knife-edge drafts all winter. Some day I'll shingle the whole thing."

Their honeymoon of rain was over, all the good hours together, the little jokes, the talk, the excitement of fixing up their house side by side. Molly had not seemed to miss her family at all while it rained and now she still did not go to see them while Dave worked near the house and she could catch a glimpe of him from the kitchen window cleaning up the garden for the winter or could call to him as she hung her dishcloths on the line and have him call back between brisk hammering along the side of the barn where he was nailing ten-foot strips of wood over the cracks between the old boards. The barn had probably been fairly tight when it was built forty years earlier, but the wood had

shrunk, and from inside one could see long slits
of light on every hand, excellent for ventilation,
but hard on the animals tied and almost motionless through the long winter days and longer
nights.

Molly liked to have Dave working near at
hand, but when Chip came over one morning to
borrow the team and the blue-wheeled cart to
haul the firewood he had been cutting back in
the woods, and Dave insisted upon going along
to help, Molly went off for the day with her
family.

"You ring the farm bell when you come back,"
she said, "and I'll be right along. I can hear
it down the wind."

Dave made no objection, but he would be
glad when Molly got so she could stay at home
like other women while her husband went off
about his natural affairs. He said something to
Chip about it, not exactly in criticism, but showing his mind, and the older man gave his usual
answer, "You're in too much of a hurry, Dave.
Give the girl time. She's doing real well, if you
ask me."

And when Dave said something more, Chip
added: "You can't have everything. I've lived a
long time and I ain't seen perfection yet."

It was towards the end of the week that one afternoon a car came up the Dead River Road. It was small and shining, a town car, natty, without a dent or scratch on its mudguards. At sight of it, Chip made his appearance, and so did the black cat and most of the hens. Molly ran to the kitchen window and Dave, who had been digging potatoes, straightened his back and listened to the sound of the motor, as the car drew up to his own dooryard.

"Must be lost," he thought. "I'd better go and give him directions."

When he got around to the back door, Molly had already opened it and invited the man in. With a leap of his heart, Dave recognized Ed Jordan, the manager from the lumber office. They shook hands heartily, standing in the kitchen.

"No one would guess what this place looked like in May," Mr. Jordan said. "And I see you've found time to get married. That's the right way to begin, isn't it, Mrs. Ross?"

"Won't you come into the parlor?" asked Molly with her pretty smile. She was wearing one of her sprigged dresses and looked old-fashioned and trim as usual, and Dave felt proud of her appearance and of her ease with a stranger.

Her manners were always simple and kind. He could see that Mr. Jordan was quite impressed by Molly.

But after all, he was a manager and his business was not in the parlor nor in talking to Mrs. Ross, although he noted with approval the neat appearance of both. A sound farmhouse often makes a sound farm, and he liked the look of this one. Ross was an intelligent fellow he could see, not going off half-cocked like some young men.

Mr. Jordan bowed to Molly.

"I'd like to, but some other time, Mrs. Ross. I'm hoping that your husband will show me around the place. I noticed your mares, Ross. I'd like to see them closer if you have time."

"Certainly, sir," said Dave. "But won't you come back for supper? There's no place to get anything to eat nearer than Skowhegan that I know of."

"Yes, do," chimed in Molly and Ed Jordan accepted with evident pleasure.

Dave had been thinking quickly what there was in the house. Plenty of vegetables from their garden; Molly had churned that week; he knew how good her biscuits and puddings were.

"I'll be with you in a few minutes," he said to Mr. Jordan and going out, caught three of the young chickens and chopped off their heads at the old block. Since his marriage, he had never killed any of the broilers. Molly seemed set against it and in his comparative inexperience, he himself wasn't anxious to do it. He'd put it off until some occasion should arise. Well, it had arisen now, and his part was over.

He put the three chickens in the sink and joined Molly and Mr. Jordan. The two men tramped across the kitchen, the stranger going first. Dave paused to say to Molly:

"I've left three broilers for supper."

She gave one agonized look at the bleeding bodies in the sink and turned white. Her eyes were desperate.

"I don't know how," she whispered.

When Dave came to the farm, he hadn't known how to do things either, but he had done what *he* had to do. Why shouldn't she?

"It's time you learned," he replied, low so that Ed Jordan shouldn't hear, but with a certain suppressed anger. Suddenly he was sick of coddling Molly. Let her behave like other people! And he turned without looking at her again, and went out, shutting the door behind him.

For nearly two hours he tramped with Ed Jordan over the place. They inspected the horses, about which the lumberman was well informed. He gave Dave some good advice, discussed lumber horses, and the qualities needed, and recommended certain salves and remedies which his company has found efficacious in their many years of experience. He was, of course, especially taken by Alice.

"You'll have a good colt there," he said. "I'm not so sure how that lady will work out," he added, looking hard at Daisy-Belle, who arched her neck and looked back at him blandly. "She's pretty, but I never like a horse with four white socks and a long back. Still, the colt may be all right. This big gold-digger here looks good," and he gave Skowhegan Sue's long nose, thrust over the fence, a knowledgeable rub. The work team, too, came in for their share of attention. Ed Jordan was sizing up the condition of the coats of all the horses, and of their tempers. No man can disguise ill-treating a horse, but these, except old Alice, were all gentle, "clever," as the saying goes, and not headshy. Alice's surliness, his quick eye knew, was of long standing. For a beginner, Ross had done very well.

They walked slowly over the hayfields and pastures, Dave showing what he had done and meant to do. The sparrows spattered out of the

grasses as they approached, taking soil and lime, and ditching junipers and such matters. A partridge suddenly whirred up from a clump of alders with a sound like a small explosion, and the young roosters were cheerfully crowing back and forth between Dead River Farm and Chip's shack.

All the time the river's brightness shone below the fields, and its voice was never still. The forest stood gravely on the opposite shore. It rose, too, behind the barn and the upper field, protecting and threatening the clearing. A fox yapped and another fox answered.

"There must be good shooting here," remarked Ed Jordan. "Do you mind if I bring my bird dog some day next month and see what we can scare up? Perhaps you'll come along?"

Dave admitted that he had no gun and had never hunted. But Mr. Jordan must come.

"Beyond here the land hasn't been touched for four or five years. It's all overgrown and I imagine there's good cover."

Their last visit was to the barn. If the lumber teams came here for the summer, they would not spend any time under a roof, but there were usually a few sick or lame horses which had to be laid off during the working season for a few days or weeks.

"You'd better learn as much as you can, Ross, about horse diseases. Go in and see the veterinarian, Thomson, in Skowhegan. You can learn a lot from talk. And he can tell you the right books to read."

"I know him," said Dave. "He helped me choose the team and the old mare you like. Then Chip Chandler, who's been a blacksmith at the camps and lives over there, has had a lot more experience than I've had. He's a good neighbor and always ready to help out."

Ross knows enough to know he doesn't know everything, Jordan thought. He'll do. And aloud he reaffirmed his promise to send as many horses to Dead River as the farm could handle. The two men sat down on the back steps and talked money. Dave was satisfied with the board the company was willing to pay.

"I'll write you a letter tomorrow confirming this," Jordan said. "You ought to have it down in black and white. You say you've feed for five or six more horses this winter? I may take you up on that."

In mutual good humor the men rose to go into the kitchen from which issued the smell of broiling chickens and baking powder biscuits.

But it was not Molly who turned from the

stove as they entered, but the small, weather-worn figure of Chip Chandler, wearing an apron. Introductions took place and then explanations.

"Molly had word of trouble at home, Dave," Chip explained, "and she had to go. Clotilde was took with an ache or something. She asked me could I take over and I said, 'Gladly.' I guess things are about ready to dish up."

This was so much eye-wash and Dave knew it. Molly had not liked the look of those damned chickens and had run home to Mama, but although he felt his irritation rising, he hid it before company. But for once Molly should have a piece of his mind when he brought her home, and during most of the meal he took part in the talk somewhat absent-mindedly, while he thought up things to say to Molly when they would be alone. If he were more absorbed in his plate than usual, Chip was equal to the occasion and he and Mr. Jordan reminisced about the Enchanted until gradually Dave was drawn back into the present.

It was not until nearly ten that evening that the manager drove away, calling back, "I'll write tomorrow morning."

Chip lighted his pipe.

"Sure, Dave," he said soothingly, "them Perdrys never had chickens. The child didn't know what to do with them. You mustn't fly off the handle at her for that. I saw her rocketing down the road when you two were in the upper pasture, and I thought maybe it was time for me to put in an appearance. I heard them chickens squawking when you was chasing them and knowing Molly, I put two and two together."

He made light of Dave's thanks, but before he left, the old man looked at his neighbor with unexpected earnestness.

"You go slow," he warned. "You don't understand all about Molly's bringing up, yet. Just be patient. Don't you be in a hurry, Dave."

It wasn't, however, because of Chip's warning that Dave didn't go to the Perdrys' that night. When he was alone, he felt suddenly tired out. Ed Jordan's coming had been like an examination of himself and of all his works. And then Molly's desertion and his own wave of anger had about finished him. The Perdrys would be in bed and Dave didn't relish waking them up and making a scene. He'd go down in the morning, if she didn't come home under her own steam.

Half in anger, half in loneliness, Dave undressed and went to bed. When he had blown out the lamp, he looked out from the west window to see if he could catch a glimpse of lamp-light through the alder thicket between his land and the Perdrys'. But all was darkness and the clouds had come in since sundown and covered the stars.

OCTOBER

When Dave woke up a sense of joy pervaded him. For perhaps half a minute he tasted that universal well-being of the spirit roused from refreshing sleep. The sick man for that little space feels no pain nor heaviness; the debtor has not yet picked up the heavy burden of worry which lies at his feet; the heart has forgotten its sorrow.

But pain and trouble and grief are waiting, and Dave's eyes, at first focused with blind content on the pale ceiling overhead, swept slowly across the well-known room and then, with a turn of his head, swung to the pillow beside him. No sleek brown head lay upon it with a braid over each young shoulder, no dark eyes looked smilingly into his, no voice asked, "Time to get up?" with a little rising, almost singing inflection.

Dave's dismay and anger closed in about him. He fought his way into his clothes, and tramped heavily through the sunny parlor and into the kitchen. He had some vague boyish hope that Molly might be there, getting breakfast, but the room was empty and untidy, last night's dishes lying helter-skelter everywhere, with the bones and skins of the broilers spread in unappetizing abandon beside half-eaten biscuits and left-over cauliflower and potatoes.

Dave started the fire, banging about a great deal more than usual, and went out to milk while the coffee in the old blue pot heated to a boil. It was as he was coming with the milk pail out of the barn door, which faced south towards the river, that he saw something which profoundly worried him. He had put the horses in the lower pasture, across the road, and as usual his eye glanced over them to make sure that everything was all right and that Alice did not need his help. But this morning his eye checked suddenly on a stranger. It was the Perdrys' old black, hobbling along cheerfully with the others, grazing when they grazed and raising its whitening head when they raised theirs. Never had the Perdrys put the creature in with his stock, and instantly Dave knew that its presence portended something.

He hurried through his breakfast, mostly standing beside the stove, and giving the dishes a look of distaste, went out, slamming the door behind him. His violence startled some crows catching grasshoppers and crickets in front of the house and they beat up against the blue sky, the strong sunlight slanting white on their wings.

The chickens in their yard made a great breakfast outcry as they saw him, complaining and calling, but he went on. From the alders, flocks of vesper sparrows flew out, the gray and white stripes of their tails spread like little fans and in the mud of the road where it was always wet with the overflow of the alder spring, he saw the small handlike tracks of raccoons, and thought of the hens, without however checking his stride.

The Perdry house was empty. No smoke rose from its chimney and the windows had the blind look of a house without occupants. For no reasonable reason Dave tried the door and found it open. It was the same door by which Molly had stood that evening and reached out her hand to him in the darkness.

The house was very empty inside. It was in a general way neat, but there were many signs of recent occupancy, a pipe laid down half-filled on the table, a punctured can of milk on the sink, an apple bitten into and laid aside. The bedrooms with their crowded cots continued the same story, in shoes kicked into the corners, and ties and towels left out of place. But none of the beds had been slept in, and the kitchen stove, whose ashes showed not the least glow of life, told the same tale.

Dave knew in which room Molly had slept with Clotilde before her marriage, and sure enough on the rickety bureau under the cheap mirror he saw a small spray of leaves and berries, not as fresh as they always seemed in her hair, but dried up, with the red berries pinched-looking and withered. There was no message, however, and none on the tables downstairs or pinned to the back door or the front. No one had walked through the grass since the dew had fallen, but himself.

Jaunty, devil-may-care, with its fringed canopy faded and askew, the surrey stood beside the house, its shafts pointing into the ground.

Dave knew that it was no use, but something too profound to be resisted forced him to shout, "Molly!" again and again. The Enchanted muted his calls like velvet. There was no echo. But at last the crows cawed back an ironic answer, and sick at heart, Dave was silent.

Long ago he had been angry with Chip Chandler for his hints about the Perdrys, his vague, perhaps mad, assumptions which Dave had never quite wished to fathom. But the old woodsman had been a good friend, and he had shown towards Molly a sort of amused tenderness. Now Dave hurried to the tar-paper shack and found Chip already lounging peacefully on the doorsill with the black cat sitting tall and drowsy below him on the sunny step.

"Hello," said Dave, and Chip answered:

"Hello. Fine day, ain't it?" and moved over to make room for Dave beside him. Dave sat down, pushing the cat off the step. He said nothing.

The little lumberman was also silent for a while, and then between puffs at his pipe, he remarked:

"See the Perdrys put that old black crowbait in your pasture."

"Yes," said Dave, and then in a rush he exclaimed, "They've all cleared out!"

Chip nodded and went on smoking.

"Molly too?"

Dave threw up his hands without speaking.

"I ain't surprised," Chip said mildly. "I've seen it coming on a long time. They've been getting restless. But I thought maybe Molly had settled down. It's too bad Molly went with them."

"You bet it's too bad!" Dave cried savagely. "What are they, anyhow—gypsies?"

And he stared at Chip, who continued to look down towards the river.

"Well, not exactly gypsies," he began, but Dave interrupted.

"Look here!" he said. "I can't stand any more hints. Tell me right out what you know. I want to know about Molly. I feel as if I'd go crazy."

But the lumberman continued his quiet smoking.

"Dave," he said at last, "you don't ask your questions at the right time. There's a right time and a wrong time for most things. This here's the wrong time. If you'd asked in June, I'd have told you and you'd have said I was a crack-brained idjit. Now you might believe me or you might not, but either way I'm not going to tell you. Besides, I don't know anything. I just think.

And I'm not a man like you with an education. I'm just an old lumberman past my working days, who's spent most of his life in the Enchanted."

And Chip turned his head over his shoulder to stare at the woods, whose outer wall shone in lemon and bronze and scarlet and rich pine green in the sunlight across the fields, but whose shadows lay forever unpierced not twenty feet from the open land.

"Then there's no use talking." Dave got to his feet. He had hoped for help, but it was something he'd have to work out, or Molly would. He didn't know.

But Chip wasn't quite through, it seemed.

"Don't you go putting in one of them notices in the paper about how since your wife, Molly Ross, has left your bed and board, you ain't responsible for any bills she may run up," he called after Dave with a certain effort towards joviality. "She won't run any bills, and she might turn up any minute. You can't tell."

Dave swung back.

"You think she will?"

"I don't know really. It looks to me about fifty-fifty."

"Well, so long," said Dave.

"So long," said Chip. And the cat came back

and sat down on the step, as though it had left it for a few minutes not through the will of another, but entirely on some errand of its own.

The following days saw Dave grimly at work. He made the barn tight and then began housing up, putting on the storm windows downstairs, and banking the sills with green balsam boughs in a long garland. The rats and mice were beginning to come into the house, getting ready for winter, and every evening he reset the traps, and most mornings found at least one of them filled. The same instinct for seeking shelter had seized upon the flies, and he hung fly-strips from the kitchen ceiling near the stove and sink.

The days were still warm, but the nights were getting cold and he brought the stock into the barn now at sundown. The first night he hesitated when the old black horse came with the others. He had an impulse to drive it off, to hit at it with a stick, but he could not do it. He let it in with the rest, gave it a stall, and some oats.

In the evenings which followed, he found himself often standing in front of the tie-up watching the old creature's satisfaction as it ate. He gave it as much as the others, sometimes even more. It was food wasted. The old horse was done for, but it was so happy to have care

again! As its ribs began to fill out, it stepped along in a more lively fashion, and once in the field Dave surprised it nipping at one of the mares in rusty playfulness.

"Hi! Stop that!" he shouted, heaving a pebble at the offender, but he grinned for the first time in some days, and that evening he curried the black with the others.

The days went on, all mild, all golden. Chip said he had never seen such an October. The bluebirds came, stayed a few days, calling from the orchard, and passed southward: waves of robins came and were gone. The partridges' note sounded from the fields, and the deer began to come boldly into the open land. More than once he saw them wading in the shallows along the edge of the river, outlined on its quicksilver, and his cabbages suffered from their visits at night.

One evening when Dave went to call in the horses, he saw a strange, ungainly form among them which followed for a few steps with the stock and then stood as though hesitating.

Dave saw that it was a moose.

"No," he said to the creature, "I draw the line on moose."

He had begun getting in his winter wood in earnest now, and several times on the old

tote road he met a bear which looked at him
from its little inquisitive eyes and shambled off
out of sight. These long days of hard work, and
their beauty, and the shadowy neighbors which
came to him out of the sky and out of the im-
measurable woods, had their comfort for Dave,
but all the time he felt empty with loneliness.
Sometimes he thought about Molly and sometimes he only missed her without conscious
thought. Long ago his anger had burned out like
a fire which cannot feed upon itself, but the
hurt remained.

He finished painting the inside of the house
during a spell of east wind and rain. One day
he took Chip with him on a trip to Skowhegan
and came back with a square of tin to block off
the fireplace, and a parlor stove.

Another afternoon a great flock of wild geese
came honking out of the north and passed over
his roof in a series of four or five wedges which
joined to the south into one long fluctuating rib-
bon, curled back at its ends, which grew fainter
and fainter and at last was gone. That night
Dave went for Chip and by the light of two
lanterns they saw Alice through her labor. Even
when they lifted her colt to its feet and the mare
stood with her big head drooped over its neck,

she kept her sullen look. No light of tenderness brightened her eye, no excitement pointed her ears forward.

"But look out for her heels!" said Chip. "She's on guard over her little fellow just the same. And ain't he a beauty!"

Even Dave could see that the colt was good. He looked at the wobbly little thing with pride and affection. This was his first real return on the labor he had put into the farm. The fencing, the haying, the ditching and the rest had all led up to this newborn creature, and had been for this, and for this alone.

"We'll call him 'Dead River Dan'!" he thought. The name had sprung into his head. If the colt had been a filly, he had meant to name it "Enchantress." But as it was, this little horse should be called after the farm.

"Dead River Dan," he repeated out loud, and Chip said:

"That's a good name."

They went into the kitchen and made themselves coffee. The fire was hot in the stove, and the kettle had been refilled and was boiling again, and the strong smell of hot bran mash hung in the air. They drank their coffee, still talking a little excitedly. They had been helping nature in its most essential work and things had gone well. The faces of both men showed a strong satisfaction.

But when the door closed behind Chip, the old loneliness swept over Dave. He wanted to call into the room across the hall:

"Get up, Molly, and put on your coat. I've got something to show you," but he knew that the room was empty and that no one would answer if he called. Wherever Molly was, she was beyond the reach of his voice. Clumsy with sudden weariness, he picked up his lantern and went again into the barn to make sure that all was well. When he got to bed, he left on his underclothes and put the lantern, turned low, on the chair beside him. He would be in and out for the rest of the night. He wanted to take no chances of any harm's coming to Dead River Dan now in the frail hours of his extreme infancy.

The days went slowly by and the housing up was nearly completed. Dave brought in his poles of shell beans and put them in the barn loft; a little more cold weather and he could cut the cabbages and store them in the cellar. They were shaped like huge old-fashioned roses, and their outer leaves, whose sea-green was flushed with purple, were so strong that they never stirred when the sparrows lighted on them in their search for feeding insects.

One day he decided to finish his autumn plowing. The land he planned to put to corn next year lay on the upper slope, where his line ran along Chip Chandler's. He worked all morning, went home, started up the fire, fed the team, heated some of his own baked beans, and as he returned, looked at his furrows with some satisfaction. They were straight and even, but he felt that a good deal of the praise belonged to Pat and Patience, who were well-accustomed to the work, and well-trained to obey their driver's voice. Dave was able to work with the reins behind his neck, which left both hands free for the plow.

It was about two in the afternoon when he heard a car coming through the woods on their road. No stranger had been along it since Ed Jordan's visit on the day Molly left, and Dave remembered the manager's promise to come back some day with his dog and a gun. But as the car came out into the fields, slowly because of the condition of the ruts, Dave saw that it was unknown to him, and that he had never before seen the middle-aged driver in his red-and-black-checked shirt and red cap. If the man's clothes had not already marked him for a hunter, the Gordon setter on the seat beside him would have told the story.

Seeing Dave in the field, the stranger waved, and Dave, still lunging along the emerging furrow, raised one hand briefly in return. He saw the man draw up by the side of the road and get out followed by his dog, and for a while he followed their figures in the river field before they were lost to view among the alders. Usually there were plenty of partridges about, but on this day they seemed to have vanished. Some time passed, and the plowing was almost finished, and Chip's black shack stood bright in the westering radiance of the afternoon when Dave heard two or three shots fired in quick succession. They filled the clearing with their sudden tearing of the silence and then the sounds dropped away and were gone, and Dave soon forgot again the hunter and his hunting as he worked.

The shadows of the Enchanted beyond the Perdrys' had lengthened until they covered all the fields. Only in the sky the last rich light still lay along the clouds, and a small flock of late robins overhead seemed to have breasts of fire, while all the earth lay below them, subdued and somber in its own shadow.

Dave unfastened the plow at the end of the

furrow. One more thing was finished, but he would get the plow under cover tomorrow, not tonight. His back ached, and his arms were tired, and his legs felt of different lengths from walking half in the furrows and half out, pushing down the clods as they turned up like obstinate surf. He was tired, and with the dusk the dark presences of the Enchanted and of his loneliness always seemed to return doubly upon him. He took the reins from his stiff neck and unfastened the horses from the plow. They were less tired than he or more hungry. For them, the barn held only pleasant associations and they started for home at a quickened pace, tossing their heads against the restraint of the bits.

Dave heard the car and drove the impatient team well to the side of the road and pulled them to a halt. The stranger slowed down as he went by.

"Nice horses," he said.

"How was the hunting?" Dave asked.

"Rotten," said the man. "I started one covey and I'm sure I winged a bird, but it got away."

"Too bad." In the dusk, Dave noticed that the dog sat guiltily as though it were somehow a party to failure. Then the car drove on, and the team strode back into the road, their necks bent and their heads held low against the drag

136

of the man who controlled them. Darkness comes quickly in late October and already the new moon, which had been a cloud-colored wraith among the clouds, shone bright like a sickle of steel in the west. The windows of the farm showed pale yellow with the uncertain shine of lamps lighted before the final coming of night. Dave stared at them and for a moment his mind turned numb. He could not think what the lights meant, so natural and simple did they seem in themselves, yet so utterly unexpected.

"Maybe Chip's dropped in about something and lighted up," he thought, but Chip had never done such a thing before. He let the horses have their heads and they walked faster and faster, almost at the edge of a trot, and Dave hurried after them. As he turned up the drive he heard the voices, the many cheerful low voices which he knew so well and had expected never to hear again. At the back steps he threw the reins over the horses' haunches and left the team to their own devices while he ran up the steps and flung open the kitchen door.

A hubbub of voices greeted him, and someone threw herself into his arms. It was Molly and her face was wet with tears.

"I wanted to come back, but I couldn't until

they did," Dave heard her voice, but he didn't
have time to answer her before they were all
crowding round him and Papa Perdry was patting him on the shoulder in the old way. There
had been several times during the last weeks
when Dave would gladly have strangled Papa
Perdry, but not now. Mama Perdry was patting
his other shoulder. "Dear boy, how have you
been?" and all the boys and girls pressed about,
in that wave of affection and family warmth for
which his heart suffered.

He tried to voice his long-held anger and de-
spair, but he was so happy to see them that all
he could find to say was "Where have you been?
Why didn't you let me know?"

And even this was drowned in a dozen cheerful answers, no two of them alike, and the loving laughter of a family enjoying a family joke.
They were all back. The good days had returned. The happy-go-lucky, hand-to-mouth,
kindly, improvident gang was back again. They
would answer no questions, make no explanations nor apologies, their role was simply to be,
and Dave knew that he must accept them on
their own terms or not at all. And accept them
he did, glad to have them back again. But he
had been too deeply hurt by Molly to recover

so quickly after the long ache of emptiness. His anger awoke in its ashes. He said nothing and his face was expressionless as he looked at her in quick, almost stealthy glances.

But in the confusion no one seemed to notice. "Come along! supper's ready!" Mama Perdry called in her pretty singing voice. "Come along, Dave. We've put the big chair at the head of the table for you, and Molly will sit beside you."

It was like the housewarming dinner. There were even the same deep-scented pine boughs in the corners of the room and the fresh green wreath over the mantel.

Dave sat down, half in a dream. They all looked the same, round, bustling and merry. The same black, rather expressionless eyes looked back into his, the same low banter and laughter filled the room. Only Molly was different. Confused as his feelings were, he was very aware of her. She wore her sprigged gingham, and the little bunch of leaves and berries was still in her wavy hair, but now they were not needed to distinguish her at a glance from Sally, Anna and Clotilde. Probably the change had been coming on for a long time, all summer, but he had lived too close to her to notice. The shape of her face seemed different and the lines of her brow no longer were exactly like her sisters'. But above all, the new thing lay in her expression, which continually varied from moment to moment, now gay, now serious, but always with a slight uncertainty about it which it had never had before. When Molly's anxious glance met his, the quality of her eyes themselves struck him as not the same. The large dark irises had lost their opaqueness, and he looked for the first time deep into them.

But the friendly talk beat against his attention.

"I'm afraid there wasn't much to make a dinner of," he apologized, but they laughed at him.

"Oh, we can live on bread and tea for weeks and be perfectly happy," Mama Perdry answered for the family. "Wait till you see what we've found. And there are two apple pies browning in the oven at this minute."

"How's the old horse?" asked Matt, and Dave reported that it was fat and frisky.

"I make you a present of him, Dave, my boy!" exclaimed Papa Perdry expansively. "We've no barn and no hay, you know, so I give him to you outright."

Dave grinned. "I'm surely grateful, sir," he said and he was, with his fingers crossed, maybe.

If the barn should catch fire—that worst dream of every stock farmer—it would probably be old Blackie he'd try to get out first, although all reason and sense would be against it.

But Mama Perdry exclaimed:

"Don't take him too seriously, Dave. He'll want to borrow Blackie the minute we have to go to town."

"But the surrey won't be any more use after snow comes," said Clotilde.

That raised an outcry. "Don't you remember the old sleigh at the deserted farm just before you come to the Forks—way at the back of that fallen-in barn? It even has bells on the shafts."

"It will only hold two or three," argued Clotilde.

"That will be big enough, my dears," said Papa Perdry a little sadly. "You're scattering in the next few weeks, you know. Yes, Dave," he went on, "this is our last family reunion for a while. The young people have all met someone they care for, and they won't be under our roof much longer."

Dave was rather taken aback by this wholesale announcement.

"Well, congratulations, all of you!" he cried. "Here's to long life and happiness all around the table!" and raising his cup of coffee, he drank to them collectively, while they bowed and smiled in return.

"I'm going to live on Lower Enchanted Pond," said Clotilde. "Our grandpapa used to live there."

Matt said, "We're not going so far back. I think we'll settle at Camp No. 5."

"That's the clearing we went through on our honeymoon," Molly explained in an aside to Dave. "Of course, the camp, itself, is gone now."

"We mean to stay here," said Anna. "Down by the river."

The others told where they were going. It had an epic quality, this scattering of a family to find new homes in the wilderness, but no one seemed at all afraid, timid as Dave had always thought them.

"There'll be quite a colony of us," Dave said, imagining the new roofs which must be built before winter and the smoke from at least two more chimneys which would drift across the fields on a winter's morning. But the family, which was in high spirits, laughed at him in their friendly secretive way.

"You won't be seeing much of us, Dave," giggled Anna, and Jasper repeated, "No, you won't see much of us, Dave."

"Well, I'd better hold tight to Molly," Dave said, trying to joke, but still with that coldness in his voice which returned almost against his will whenever he spoke to her.

"I'll never leave you again, as long as you want me, Dave," she said eagerly. "I'll be all right now."

She was not laughing, and Mama Perdry was not laughing either when she said:

"Yes, Dave, she brought us back. She doesn't belong to the Enchanted anymore. She belongs to you and your people now."

Dave thought, why, Molly looks like Mama Perdry, or perhaps it was Mama Perdry who looked a little like Molly.

"Well, here's to us all!" cried Jasper, and he lifted his own cup high in his left hand.

"Here's to us all!" the others repeated, but Dave's attention suddenly focused on Jasper's right arm, which until then he had not noticed in the crowd of people about the table. It was neatly bandaged and held in a sling.

A sudden sense of shock, out of all proportion to the occasion, numbed Dave's mind.

"What did you do to yourself, Jasper?" he asked slowly.

And immediately the answers ran around the table, in the usual bantering fashion:

"He was climbing a tree and fell out."

"He was milking your cow and she kicked him."

"Blackie didn't recognize him and bit him."

"No, no, it was a widow-maker caught in another young tree. It sprang back and scraped his forearm when he was chopping firewood."

"He was attacked by a chipmunk, Dave."

Jasper grinned and said:

"I stopped some birdshot. A fool was shooting down in the alders and didn't see me coming up the path."

Suddenly, Dave's long questioning and the doubting, incredible answers from which his mind had turned blindly away were at an end. Clearly and simply, he saw the truth at last.

And all at once with that realization a curious thing happened to him. The crowded table before him faded and the sound of voices changed and he thought that he was standing in one of the glades of the Enchanted with the forest dark about him, rising up denser and taller than trees should rise. There he stood waiting, waiting for something which was moving towards him from a long distance off. Someone else was with him, at his shoulder. He could not see who it was without turning his head, but he

was aware that he was not alone and that there were two people waiting in the same suspense for the approach of some presence or power which filled him with terror and wonder and yet which he had no hope nor even wish to escape. And about his feet there were low sounds and slight, almost imperceptible motions, but he did not look down to see what caused them, all his attention being focused upon the darkness of the forest and the unhurried yet soundless approach which he felt from its depths. And at last, as the suspense became almost unendurable, he heard a sound from a direction he had not expected and knew it for what it was, the Voice of the Enchanted, and turning to face it, swept his arm out to push Molly farther behind him, for now he knew that his companion was Molly.

Dave's outflung hand swept glass and plates to the floor with a terrific crash and the sound of the partridges which had been at his feet in the glade and of the Perdrys scattering from the table blended into one confusion, bringing Dave back to the present and his own home. Only Dave did not stir from his chair, only he and Molly. For Molly, with her hands on the edge of the table in the very act of pushing back her chair with the others, had stopped, and, fixing her eyes rigidly on Dave's face, waited for him to act.

"I beg your pardon," he exclaimed to everyone. "I must have been dreaming. I'll get the dust pan, Molly. What a mess!"

But Papa and Mama Perdry and all the others were laughing.

"We know that kind of dream!" Mama Perdry said. "Why, we've been living in that kind of dream for months and months. Then we wake up and are ourselves and then the dream comes back. But you're different."

"Yes, he's like Chip. It can't get hold of him," Papa Perdry agreed.

"And Molly's like him now." Mama looked at Molly proudly. "It can't get hold of her anymore either."

"It doesn't want to or it could," Anna argued. They were all sitting at the table again. "It's changed her for good the way it does sometimes."

"No," said Mama. "She's changed herself. She finished changing while we were away."

Jasper was laughing.

"Dave knows! I see it in his eye. When did you guess, Dave?" and they all laughed together, staring intently at him with their round expres-

sionless eyes at once so gentle and so impenetrable.

"When I saw your arm in a sling, Jas."

All the questioning was over. The incredible
had happened and he believed it, as Chip had
believed it long ago. His reason no longer
fought to establish itself, to force the dark law-
less world of the Enchanted to obey its laws.
Perdry? Wasn't that something like the word
for partridge, in French? He had known a man
named Partridge once, Jim Partridge. But these
people were *really* partridges, and perhaps because the Enchanted had touched his eyes, the
fact seemed to Dave no more important than if
they had said that they were gypsies. He was not
even surprised. Perhaps he was too surprised to
realize it yet. That might come later.

It was not Dave but Molly, who had never before taken any responsibility for the outside
work, who now noticed the sound of the horses
pawing at the hollow floor of the barn, waiting
to be unharnessed and let into their stalls.

"I'll go," she exclaimed, jumping to her feet.
"I'll just light the lantern. We've forgotten
them, poor things."

"Oh, let them wait, it won't hurt them! We
want to talk," chorused the young people. But

148

Molly looked up with a new pride, snapping the big chimney carefully into place over the wavering light.

"That's what *they* think," she exclaimed to Dave and smiled at him as their eyes met.

He opened the door and stood back a little to let her go by, but as he closed it again behind them, he found that her mood had shifted and that she was half crying as she put her free hand on his arm, looking up into his face in the starlight, the lantern bright at their knees.

"Now you know all about me, Dave," she faltered. "Everyone guessed, even Chip's cat. Only you didn't know."

"Why did you come back?" he asked, not touching her.

"Because I loved you so much."

Still he said nothing, and now she insisted desperately against his silence.

"Please understand, Dave. You thought I was a girl when I wasn't. But now I *am* a girl, whatever the others may still be. Don't think I'm not, when now at last I am!"

"But I don't understand," he began.

And again she said, in that new voice of hers, "Oh, it was hard—but because I loved you—and the baby was coming—" He heard her voice pleading with him to be forgiven for being what she was or had been. And suddenly some conception of all that she had dared for his sake came to him. Alone, gentle and timid, dependent upon the covey for her security, she had dared loneliness and womanhood to be with him. The memory, not of her small failures, but of her brave successes flamed through him. Now with horror and admiration he saw her fighting the crouching and determined cat, now measured the solitary hours in the kitchen, and understood her trembling and poignant pride as she milked the cow. And all because she loved him.

"Don't, don't, Molly," he said, shaken at last, his arms heavy about her, his face against hers. "I know now. I understand. Forgive me for not understanding before."

"But how could you?" she excused him.

And still in his arms, once more her mood veered and she began to laugh, not as the Perdrys laughed in low chuckles, but out loud, and Dave, relieved from the long tension of the summer and this evening's sudden enlightenments, began to laugh with her, while from the depths of the Enchanted an echo answered them, mocking and fastidious.

October

But hand in hand, without so much as a glance at the forest, they moved towards the barn, and the horses, hearing their slow footsteps, turned their heads over their shoulders and whinnied impatiently.